R.J. Quilantan

JASPER
The Summer Solstice at Stonehenge
A COTSWOLD STORY

SALTO AL REVERSO

JASPER
The Summer Solstice at Stonehenge
A Cotswold Story

Copyright © Rodolfo Jose Quilantan Tapia
Mexico City, Mexico, 2022

SALTO AL REVERSO

First edition: May 2022
Cover Illustration: Faörie
Collection Design: Carlos Papaqui

All rights reserved. This publication may not be reproduced, in whole or in part, or registered or transmitted in any form or by any means without the author's prior written permission.

This is a work of fiction. All the characters, organizations, and events portrayed in this novel are either product of the author's imagination or are used fictitiously. Any resemblance to actual persons, living or dead, or locales is entirely coincidental.

To those who believe in magic.

*To my father and mother,
who have always supported me.*

CONTENTS

FOREWORD		13
PREFACE		15
AUTHOR'S NOTE		17
1	The Village	19
2	Old Crazy Maggie	24
3	The Dream	34
4	The Summer Solstice	38
5	The Omen	50
6	Uneasiness at Home	55
7	Back to Cirencester	58
8	Distress in the Forest	66
9	Maeve	78
10	The Truth	90
11	Leaving the Village	97

12	Kemble	101
13	Jack and his Pack	106
14	Remy and Templeton 'Crackers'	117
15	Paddington Station	125
16	The Phoenix Club	133
17	Ginger the Red Squirrel	137
18	Alistair the Falcon	143
19	William	151
20	September 7th, 1940	159
21	The Escape	164
22	From Despair to Hope	175
23	Home	178
24	The Rescue	180
25	The Ritual	184
26	Oxford	189
27	Survival	194

ABOUT THE AUTHOR — 197

FOREWORD

THE MAGIC OF THE FANTASY GENRE is intertwined stupendously with the tough background of the Second World War in this novel written by R. J. Quilantan.

The beauty of the English landscapes surrounds the adventures of the protagonist of the story: Jasper, a young rabbit who, like the rest of the forest animals, has the ability to speak and even use magical resources.

The preparations for the summer solstice ceremony at the revered site of Stonehenge mark the beginning of the narrative of *JASPER–The Summer Solstice at Stonehenge. A Cotswold Story*. Accompanied by his friends Collin and Eileen, Jasper will discover a threat that looms over the fates of the forest animals, as well as over the humans.

The author skillfully describes the intensity of Jasper's visions as the central character discovers the devastating fate that the peaceful towns of the Cotswold area and the vertiginous English capital, London, will suffer from war and the threat of the fearsome falcon Alistair. In his dreams, the protagonist also foresees the danger faced by his missing older brother, William.

Through a fluid narration, Quilantan shows us colourful landscapes, ancient practices, and exciting mishaps as the three rabbits advance on a journey that will take them directly to the center of danger in search of William. Magic becomes a protective and life-saving element in the hands of the inheritors of the ancient wisdom of the druids.

On a journey full of thrilling feats, Jasper and his companions will come closer to finding the answers they desperately need. In amazement, the readers will discover the fantastic encounters of the rabbits with other animals capable of speaking and dressing as humans do: mice, foxes, owls, and squirrels are just some of the allies and opponents that the protagonists will find on their way. And they will also witness the efforts of the animals to remain hidden from the eyes of men.

The longing to return to their beloved town of Cirencester, a picturesque place that for centuries has been a haven of peace and flourishing nature, will guide the rabbits on their journey.

The author's ability to portray the bonds of friendship and loyalty between the characters is evident in each of the dialogues they exchange. Also notable are the vivid descriptions of the emotions that the three friends experience on their quest.

This is an invitation to the readers to open the doors of their imagination to the fantastic world presented by Quilantan in *JASPER*, get to know his adorable characters in depth, and get involved in their experiences. I am convinced that it is an adventure they will enjoy on every page.

Carla Paola Reyes
January 2022

PREFACE

FOR THOSE WHO HAVE NEVER been to England, the Cotswold is a small area in the southern part of the country made up of several counties and is known for their small villages and country lifestyle. Some would say it is a boring place, but others would argue it is as beautiful as an English sunset, its curvy and green hills and surrounding forests bring warmth to the soul.

The counties of Gloucestershire and Wiltshire are one of the bigger counties among the rest, and are known for having Stonehenge, the Stones of Avenbury and the beautiful town of Cirencester, where our story will begin.

Cirencester is full of history; it was the second largest town of Roman Britain after Londinium. In the first developing years of Cirencester (*Corinium Dobunnorum*) the town was a bustling place, there were shops, banks, temples, including a basilica. But as time passed, Roman Britain was no more, and Cirencester was known as *Coryn Ceasre* under Saxon rule.

After the Roman era, and during the Anglo-Saxon period, there was something peculiar that was occurring in the deep forest. There were stories and legends of druids being able to converse with the forest animals. There were rumours that, near Stonehenge, village folk would see out in the distance a person with a long beard, wearing a dark grey cloak, holding a staff, who people would refer as Merlin. And whenever people thought they saw Merlin, he would be always surrounded by a large group of small birds, big birds, red squirrels, foxes, mice, owls, badgers, sometimes wolfs and many, many rabbits.

But the common folk of those parts wouldn't dare to come close to Stonehenge or to any druid just because they were too afraid. No one knew where those stones came from, or how they got there, and no one wanted to cross a druid and be under a spell.

As time continued even further on, the concept of druids was a thing of the past and people paid less attention to the legends. Throughout the years, Cirencester adopted several beautiful and elegant architectural styles. Its narrow pathways, with the Classical, Tudor Revival, Storybook and Victorian style constructions have created a splendid and tranquil atmosphere around the town.

But, yet again there were new rumours of people hearing voices inside their shops, houses, and stables. Ordinary folk would turn around and see if it could have been children being mischievous; some other people suggested it was fairies from days of past. But that statement holds some truth to it. Though it was not fairies, it was animals of the forest that were taught the tongue of man by Merlin and the druids.

Not only did the forest creatures know how to speak the tongue, but they also dressed up to the era. But they always lived far from the humans, and they would come into town to grab food from shops, supplies for their homes and observe what is the life of humans. Every time they did so, they made sure not to be seen. Our story sets in a pivotal time of history in the 20th century, showing us how Jasper Jones had to embark on an epic journey to London, not by himself, but accompanied by trusted friends into a what seems to be total doom.

This is the tale of Jasper.

AUTHOR'S NOTE

I AM PLEASED TO SHARE my historical fantasy novel, *JASPER–The Summer Solstice at Stonehenge. A Cotswold Story.*

Allow me to transport you to the cozy village lifestyle of southern England and its deep forests in the early 1940s, where forest animals wear human clothing and can converse amongst each other. Centuries ago, at Stonehenge, the druids gifted the animals of the forest of Cirencester the ability to speak and the knowledge of magic. But they have always remained far from the sight of humans. Jasper, being the venturesome rabbit that he is, is always getting into all sorts of exploits with his best mate Collin. Unknowingly, his biggest adventure is yet to come as an evil omen appears and interrupts the summer solstice festivities. The omen shows the bombing of London, the destruction of the countryside, and the return of the spiteful Alistair the falcon that all the animals of the forest once feared.

Jasper learns that his long-lost brother William is in London with Alistair. With his fierce devotion, he decides to embark on a rescue mission with his friends, leaving the countryside to save William before London is destroyed and bringing him home. Jasper, Collin, and their other companion, Eileen, will come across several obstacles in their path. They will meet new friends and foes on their way to London and uncover the forest's hidden secrets and Jasper's family.

A whole new world of magic that yearns to be revived is being explored around southern England's quaint and peaceful villages, reflecting authentic English culture.

The target audience is middle grade and high school readers and those interested in magic, English culture, Celtic culture, and adventure.

1 THE VILLAGE

IN THE SUMMER of June 19th, 1940, war and chaos roamed continental Europe. The human war had started to spread like wildfire, creating a barren wasteland of annihilation, destruction, and death. The whole world was slowly spiralling down a vortex of sorrow, leaving behind the life that once many knew. With no hint on when the conflict may end, many endured with strength and courage.

However, for the animals of the forest of Cirencester, the conflicts of humans were of no interest to them. The summer solstice was near, and the animals were preparing for its festivities. For generations, it was quite common for the forest animals to gather at Stonehenge to receive the blessings of the summer. Mindy the mouse was in Cirencester gathering cheese from the markets, Jonathan the badger was in a human's garden collecting, or stealing, roots and vegetables, the birds would pick the berries, and Jasper would be fast asleep in his house. Now, Jasper was a young adult rabbit, with a light grey tone fur and brown eyes. He was well known amongst the rest of the forest animals; at times he would misbehave and have his fun here and there, but nothing too extreme. Always polite and always kind, his heart was in the right place. Often, he preferred to be relaxing, bathing under the sun in the presence of the forest, its tall dark green trees, the beautiful violets, and trilliums made perfect shade and a beautiful atmosphere. But when the moment called him for action, he would not shy away.

"For the love of Merlin wake up you! It's past half twelve and you haven't gotten up yet! All the animals will be at Stonehenge tomorrow evening, including Socrates the Owl, and you haven't even collected the carrots from the garden!"

Jasper rubs his eyes with his paws as he hears his mother, Catherine, nagging him to get up. He sits up from his bed and stretches, giving a big yawn.

"I'm commin, I'm commin, ma, no need to get livid so early in the morning."

"Livid?! ITS HALF PAST TWELVE! GET UP AND GET THE BLOODY CARROTS!

"Carrots coming right up, mother." Her mother walks out the room.

Catherine loved his son, but at times she had to be strict with him. Jasper, with a little bit more speed stands from the bed, grabs his brown sack coat and flat cap that settled between his ears. He passes the kitchen and sees that his mother is preparing a Victorian Sponge Cake and a Carrot Cake for tonight. As Jasper walks out the hut, he is slightly blinded by the sun, but can feel the warmth of it as well. He walks around the house to the garden and stares at the soil. He squats down and starts pulling a carrot from the stem and, instead of pulling a nice fat juicy orange carrot, he pulls out a very light orange and rather thin carrot. He takes a big sigh, already thinking on what his mother may ask of him.

"How them carrots coming along Jasper?" asked Catherine.

"Not too promising," replied Jasper, as he sighs. He grabs a wooden basket nearby and starts to collect all the carrots from their small garden. Once he gathered all of them, he returns inside the house and presents the basket to his mother, who is still working in the kitchen.

"I reckon the carrots aren't any good mum."

"Oh, dear, oh, dear tsk, tsk, this will not do, see this is why I needed you to have done this yesterday."

"You already have two cakes, mother, why do you need more carrots?"

"I have been preparing for this for a long time, Jasper, I need you to work with me here, ok? We are also bringing grilled carrots."

"How many carrots are you expecting the other animals to eat?"

Catherine just gives a straight glare to Jasper, as he is reminded not question her when it comes to the kitchen.

"Never mind," said Jasper silently as he raised his paws.

"Would you be so kindly, Jasper hunny, to go with a friend of yours, Collin maybe? And go to a human's garden and retrieve me two carrots. Just two. After this you do not have to do anything else next week, you can sleep all you want, and once everything is ready, we will head to the stones tomorrow."

Jasper nodded in agreement to get help from his mate Collin. Fortunately, Collin owes Jasper a couple of favours and knows his way around Cirencester.

Now, Collin Smith had thick shiny black fur and was one of Jaspers oldest friends, a bit too posh, but overall a good friend. The one thing that Collin took pride in was the way he dressed and his top hat. With a slight Victorian style.

Jasper was running full speed up to the highest part of the forest. As he ran, he would look up into the clear blue sky and see families of birds flying East to where Stonehenge was and the only thing on his mind were those darn carrots. As he reached the top part of the forest, he started to approach Collins family's house, and there he saw Collin on a small boulder, with his top hat covering his eyes, smoking tobacco that was stolen from the cigar shop and a small wooden pipe that was carved from the beaver family down the river.

"Who is it that I hear approaching? Ah! Jasper old bean, what brings you to this neck of the woods?"

"I need your help with something."

"Oh?" says Collin as he is blowing smoke rings.

"Mother has sent me off to go into Cirencester to retrieve two gurt carrots from one of the giant's gardens so she can cook them for the solstice festivities, but I'm not sure which house would be the easiest to get them from. Can you come with me?"

"From how I see it you have three options."

"Ok?"

"Option number one, you can risk going into the market, but right now it would be crawling with humans or child humans, and you'd risk yourself getting exposed. And you know how those child humans react when they see one of us, they are too ... joyous and I cannot comprehend why."

"Ok, so no market."

"Option number two", he takes a puff from his pipe, "you can probably go to old man's Farley's house on Ehrman Street, but rumour has it he just bought a couple of bloodhounds to guard his house, and I personally," he takes another puff, "would NOT want to be chased through Cirencester by a couple of oversized mutts.

"Agreed, that would be most undesirable. So, what is option three then?"

"Option three is not any better than option one or two, option three is going to the house of Old Crazy Maggie".

"Why do they call her Old Crazy Maggie?"

Collin laughs, "because she sworn, she'd seen us forest animals speak to each other before, but luckily the other humans don't believe her."

"Then what's the problem"? asks Jasper confusingly.

"The problem is that she is obsessed with the forest animals; she has hopes to capture someone from this forest to prove she is not mad."

Jasper just looks perplexed at Collin. "So, are you coming or not?"

"Mate, I would love to come, but you see I am terribly busy."

"Busy? Who got you out of that brawl with the Davies?"

"You."

"Who covered for you when Olivia, Lily and Freya found out you were seeing the three of them at the same time?"

"You."

"When you stole the barrels of cider and blamed it on those poor skunks? Who helped you?"

"You, you and you."

Collin takes a strong puff from his pipe trying to avoid eye contact with Jasper. "Oh, poppycock! I say we venture to option three, get those carrots for your dear mother, it shall be an adventurous journey and we will bathe ourselves in glory! By the way, is your mother making those delicious grilled carrots?"

"She's makin'em all right, too many carrots if you ask me," replies Jasper.

Both friends had started to run quickly to the main entrance of Cirencester Forest.

2 OLD CRAZY MAGGIE

COLLIN THE RABBIT was born with a silver spoon in his mouth and in a cradle made up of the finest oak that could be found in southern England. Even though being brought up in a remarkably high social class among the woodland creatures, he possessed certain attribute that many of the other animals did not. And that was the sense of adventure and exploration. He would laugh in the face of adversity and welcome it. There were times that Jasper and him were in dire situations, where they both nearly became rabbit pies, but that is another story. Not only was Collin a brave and cocky rabbit, but he was also bold, and cunning. Though Jasper was brought up in the lower middle class, he had integrity and honesty, and Collin admired him for that.

Later that day, both Jasper and Collin were at the edge of the forest. They ran towards the main gate entrance and they both stood there for a while. They could see the cathedral that stood in the town square, magnificent, tall, and strong from a distance under the bright blue sky, the clouds were white as snow and the breeze was simply perfect, the scent of English oak and flower cherries travelled through the air.

"Have you ever thought of what is beyond the village, beyond the west country?" asked Collin.

"Of course, I have, but it is a thought I rather not engage in," replied Jasper.

"Sometimes I yearn for adventure, a real exploit! An escapade if you will. Just like your brother did!"

Jasper does not reply. He just plainly looks at the distance thinking.

"Shall we go, old sport?" asked Colin as he fixed his top hat and checked that he had everything he needed from his satchel.

"It's now or never," replied Jasper.

Both rabbits rapidly ran past the gate, down Cecily Road, and hopped on to the pavement. As Jasper ran, all he could think of was not to get noticed by the humans. They both took a small break behind a tree to catch their breath. Across the street, they saw a small group of child humans walking in a line wearing their school uniforms being led by their professor. Collin was very fond of the children, he always thought they were very innocent and naïve but much cleverer than the adult humans. He felt that the children were more in tune with the magic of the forest than the adults, and he was not afraid of them. As Collin stood there, he smiled to one of them waving his top hat. As he waved, he caught the attention of a small girl as she was walking. She spotted the two rabbits in small clothing and her expression was speechless and could not believe what she was seeing.

"Miss! Miss! There's two rabbits over there and one of'em is wearing a hat and the other a jacket!"

The professor was in a hurry and did not pay much attention to her pupil.

"Come along, Shirley, we do not have time to play fairy tales at this moment."

"But the rabbits, miss!"

"I said come this instant and no more games!"

Collin was happy to be noticed by the small one, but at the same time felt a little bad because he got her in trouble.

"What on earth are you doing, you git?! You're going to get us caught!" cried Jasper.

Collin shrugged. "Apologies, old friend, the curiosity got the best of me; but how truly fascinating are the humans indeed."

Both rabbits continued their journey to Old Crazy Maggie's house and, as they ran, they were both glad that there were not as many humans on the streets as they expected to see. When they got to the end of the street, they took a hard left towards Thomas Street to get on Dollar Street where Old Crazy Maggie lives. As they approached the house both rabbits were getting a little nervous and anxious not knowing what would happen if they got caught.

The plan was to get over the wall, into the backyard, into the garden and then get out. There were a couple of empty crates by the wall that allowed both Jasper and Collin to climb onto the ledge.

When both rabbits successfully made it on the wall, they were sure to keep a safe distance from the house. They hid under the cover of branches and leaves to observe any indications if she was home or not. The coast seemed clear, so they advanced closer with much caution. They both leaped towards a tree that had branches that extended over the carrots. Collin grabbed a strong piece of rope from his satchel and tied it onto the strongest branch so they could descend into the garden.

They waited and observed any type of sign, noise, or movements from inside the house that could suggest if Old Crazy Maggie was home or not. There was a frozen silence, and they could see no movement through the stained-glass door that led into the kitchen, or anything behind the windows for that matter. After spending moments examining their situation for any indication that could impede the success of the mission, they felt it was safe and went down into the garden.

"Quickly you must go right, and I shall go left to see which are the best carrots," said Jasper. He trotted over the dirt surface sniffing and smelling at the vegetables. "Over here, over here, Jasper, come quickly," said Collin.

Jasper rapidly runs towards Collin to see him pulling out a medium size carrot from the ground and it was bright orange as the sun. "We need to get one more before we head back to the forest," said Jasper.

But they continued to look and pull the carrots from the ground, but most were not as good as the one Collin pulled out.

Collin puts his paw under his chin and starts to ponder on how they could improvise. "I say, Jasper, shall we dare wander into the house?; she must have done most of the picking of the good carrots prior to our arrival."

Jasper starts to rapidly thump his right foot onto the ground, and he starts to feel uneasy, he is thinking of whether it will be a good idea or not to enter the house. But what great tales and songs would there be about Jasper and Collin if they returned safe and sound from the house of Old Crazy Maggie. But was it worth the risk of getting caught by the monster and not knowing what could happen? For all they know, they can be cooked, boiled, baked by Maggie if things go wrong.

"Let's get the bloody carrot and quickly get home," said Jasper. Both ferociously come out of the garden onto the open grass. At this moment, they did not have any shade, bushes, or trees to hide them from sight and by the time they were a couple of meters from the door that led into the kitchen and far from their escape rope, it was already too late.

"Tee, hee, hee, oh I see you, yes I see you nice and clear." Both Jasper and Collin stopped their tracks and fear had stricken them directly into their hearts. They now realized they were in over their heads. Collin was so scared that he dropped his favourite pipe from his mouth and the carrot he had, and Jasper could only move his eyes.

They wondered where that blood-curdling voice was coming from, they could hear that petrifying laughter, but could not pinpoint her location. "Tee, hee, hee, they thought I was crazy, mad, losing the plot, but now, now I see not one, but TWO! TWO! Speaking and dressed rabbits, I'll show them! Yes!" Her malicious voice echoed and pierced the rabbit's souls.

Jasper and Collin are looking back, front, side to side hysterically wondering where she is going to appear. Both are laid onto the ground ready to disperse when she reveals herself. The door they were in front of slams wide open and, as they saw what laid before their eyes, there was a sense of overwhelming horror: the ghastly appearance of Old Crazy Maggie. She caused terror not only to the forest animals but to the rest of the residents of Cirencester. Jasper and Collin gazed upon her from head to toe, she was wearing a pair of old wellies and you could tell the colour was starting to peel off, a light pink skirt under an apron that was covered in food stains and grease, her white button shirt was not any cleaner than her face, her unpleasant face is what got to the young lads.

If someone had to tell a tale of what a witch would look like, Maggie they would say. Her nose was particularly long, uncleansed with warts all over, hair coming out her ears and nostrils, her left eye was always ticking, and her teeth rotten and dirty. Her age was around 60, but she looked over 100 years old.

"Madame human, you seem to be walking in a dream, do go back to your room and leave us be, for my associate and myself are figments of your imagination," said Collin as he tried to fool her. Jasper puts his paw over his face wondering how Collin expected that to work.

"SILLY LITTLE RABBITS! Do you take me as a fool?! A NITWIT?! I will grab both of you and show the town that I am not CRAZY! Then I will do whatever I want with you, cook you, boil you, roast you for all the embarrassment your kind has caused me!"

"Well then, I have a proposition for you," said Collin.

Old Crazy Maggie stares into the eyes of both rabbits thinking to herself, she is having a conversation with a couple of rabbits, wearing clothes, perhaps she is crazy. Listening on what Collin has to say, her breath is agitated, her lower lip is ticking. There is a small moment of silence. Jasper is waiting to see how Collin's negotiation skills will get them out of this predicament. But he isn't saying anything.

"Disperse!" yells Jasper and both rabbits run in separate directions. Collin runs to his right-hand side towards a small shed that was open, and Jasper runs in between the legs of Maggie straight into the kitchen.

"YOU DEVILS! COME BACK! ROGER! ROGEEER!"

Old Crazy Maggie calls upon her dog to fetch them. Jasper could hear Roger bark viciously on the second floor of the house knocking over everything as he was getting closer to the top of the stairway. Her dog was a white Bull Terrier that had the same crazy look as the owner. Roger descends from the stairs and immediately picks up the scent of Jasper. It was like if he entered through the gates of Hell and the animal before him was Cerberus. At this exact moment Jasper knew that he was in trouble, for one thing that scared him the most were rabid dogs.

Meanwhile, as Collin entered the shed, he saw a small stool that he could leap on that would let him hop onto one of the upper shelfs. There were several large tin cans that he could hide behind where he could catch his breath and ponder on what would be the next move. When suddenly, he could hear Old Crazy Maggie walking in the shed saying a rhyme.

> This little bunny has two big eyes.
> This little bunny is very wise.
> This little bunny is soft as silk.

Collin was able to see where Maggie was through the gap between the tin cans, and he could see she was approaching ever so slowly the upper shelf.

> The little bunny is black as night.
> This little bunny nibbles away.
> At cabbages and carrots all the livelong day!

Collin did not have much to fend himself with, only what was in his satchel. He could hear the Giant getting closer and closer and Collins's heart was starting to beat harder and harder. Then, there was silence; the whole shed went quiet.

"Such a dimwit," said Collin to himself as he realized that his top hat and ears were giving away his position, as they could be seen behind the cans.

"COME TO MUMMY!" cried Maggie as she lunged towards the shelf. Collin jumps from where he was hiding, and from his satchel, he takes out his special blend of tobacco that contained mild pepper and blew it right into her eyes to momentarily blind her. It was enough for her to yell in pain and curse Collin out, and in a berserk manner creating havoc in the shed. Collin runs out the shed knowing that this is his only chance, and quickly runs towards the house to find Jasper.

When Collin entered the house and walked in, the whole kitchen was completely upside down, everything was on the floor, messy or being destroyed by Roger as he was gnawing through the bottom cabinets trying to get to Jasper. "Help Collin! Do something!" Collin knew he had to grab the dog's attention before he would devour Jasper.

"Begone, canine from hell!" Collin yells. Roger turns his head around towards the door and sees Collin. He slowly approached him growling. The moment Roger's attention is diverted from Jasper, Jasper pops out from where he was hiding, and sees that Collin is pointing up and doing a 'shoving' gesture as if he was playing charades. Jasper looks at what he's pointing at and sees that there is a sugar pot on the edge of the counter, and now he knew what Collin was trying to get at.

"Have him chase me around the kitchen! We have one shot at this! Make it count!"

"Don't worry, I won't miss! Just make sure he gets close enough!"

Roger violently leaps towards Collin and the chase commences. As the relentless barking echoed throughout the kitchen, running across turned over chairs, flour mix, marmalade, and different types of fruit scattered everywhere, Jasper was making his way to the top of the counter. Collin had never run faster a day in his life. The moment Jasper was on the counter he places his body weight against the sugar pot so he would be ready to shove it over.

"Collin, I'm ready!"

"On my mark, when I say push you push!"

Collin was now doing laps around the kitchen with Roger getting closer and closer. He could feel the dog's hot breath behind him, closing in on him.

"Now, PUSH"!

In that moment everything turned into slow motion for both rabbits. Jasper with all his strength pushed the sugar pot off the counter that was bigger than him, and he could see the pot slowly falling towards the floor. As Collin kept on running, he looked up and saw the sugar had started to sprinkle down from above and he smiled. He looked behind him and gave Roger a grin; his face of a ferocious beast turned into confusion and tried to think why the rabbit was smiling at him. It was then that he also saw the pot falling from above. But it was too late for Roger to break in mid chase, he was running too fast, his adrenaline was too high, his ears were flapping across his head, he placed his paws in front of him trying to break but the floor was too slippery, and before it was too late the pot of sugar had landed right on Roger's head, breaking the porcelain into pieces and the sugar exploding out into the air as if someone jumped into a large pile of snow.

The lights went out in Roger's mind for the impact on his head was too hard, and he just slid across the floor unconsciously. Collin laughed aloud spreading words of victory. Jasper quickly grabbed the carrots that were on the counter and came down onto the floor to see Collin on Roger's unconscious but breathing body.

"We did it, Jasper! Hurrah, Hurrah! That'll show him never to mess about with the rabbits of the forest of Cirencester!"

"Is he dead?"

"Of course not, my dear Jasper, only gone into a deep sleep, after all we do not harm other animals, as primitive and savage as some may seem."

"I can't believe your plan worked, Collin!"

"Bob's your uncle my boy!"

Both rabbits now had for what they came for, and made their way outside to the backyard. On their left they could still see Old Crazy Maggie, blinded by the tobacco, breaking everything in the shed. Jasper just sighed at the sight of Old Crazy Maggie and decided it was best they took their leave as soon as possible before the situation could worsen.

Jasper and Collin climbed up the rope and, once they were over the wall, they both started to make their way back home with the carrots.

3 THE DREAM

AS JASPER AND COLLIN were arriving home with the carrots, many animals of the forest were leaving their homes for the celebration that would take place the next day at Stonehenge.

"Well, what took you boys so long? It's nearly dark," said Catherine.

Both rabbits just looked at each other and they began to explain the odyssey they had gone through in town.

"Jasper Jones, what am I going to do with you? Never enter a house, only a garden," said Catherine.

Collin and Jasper gave Catherine the carrots.

"Delightful! Well done, boys. While you were both gone, I baked an extra carrot cake for the both of you."

Catherine runs into the hut and brings out two individual cakes wrapped in a red and white cloth. The smell of the cakes was heavenly, and they had a dark an orange-brown colour to it.

"Brilliant! Thank you, mother," replied Jasper with much gratitude. Collin tipped his top hat in thankfulness. As polite as he could be, he said his farewells to both Jasper and Catherine and that he would be looking forward to seeing them at the ceremony tomorrow evening, and off he retreated to his abode.

"Mother, if you don't mind, I think I will rest of what is left of the day so I can wake up early to go to the stones"

"Of course, my dear, the kettle is on if you fancy yourself a cup of tea before resting," said Catherine.

A cup of tea was exactly what Jasper needed after all he went through.

Later that night Jasper had a very odd dream. He dreamt of many things that had him very confused and unaware of what was happening. He was seeing an iron eagle with its wings spread out and its head looking to the right, standing over a circle with a very peculiar sign. It looked like an 'X' but with the ends twisted in different directions. Then he had a view from the sky, as if he were flying. He saw a city, much larger than Cirencester, a place built in stone and concrete; there were buildings of different sizes with beautiful architecture that looked to have been built from another time. He saw a large river and there were several bridges crossing it. It was a sunny day with many humans walking around happily, they were all over the place that Jasper was amazed to see such large number of people walking. He saw a castle, a large tower with a clock at the very top, markets, trains, motor cars, gardens; everything looked amazing. There was so much life and enjoyment that it almost looked like a fantasy.

Out of nowhere came a large shadow covering the city. At first, he thought it was night falling or a large cloud blocking the sun. But when Jasper turned around, the sky had turned into a burnt red. There was an iron eagle that covered the sun. As he dared to stare at the cold metallic face, the eyes of the bird turned fiery red, brighter than any light that Jasper has ever seen. He had never seen such a thing and Jasper is panic-stricken and intimidated by the horror that was before him. He tries to escape the eagle by flying, but as he looked behind him, there was now a falcon. The metallic eagle had turned into a falcon of fire and gold giving a horrid screech.

Jasper feels a high temperature increasing from under him, and as he looks down at the city, of what was a view of a happy place with humans, buildings, gardens, life, movement was now a place of rubble, fire, and death. Jasper covers his eyes and screams of the atrocities that he sees.

The flames start to die off, and the smoke and ashes start to disperse. As the view starts to get clearer, down in the distance he sees a rabbit in the middle of a bridge with two towers that crosses the river. There he his, his brother William. His older brother William, the one who left some years ago abandoning Jasper and his mother, without a single goodbye. He knew that was William because he was the only rabbit that he knew that had dark blue fur with black eyes. "WILLIAM! WILLIAM! COME BACK! COME BACK HOME!" William did not respond to his cries; his only response was a stare directly into Jasper eyes and smiled. "WILLIAM! WILLIAM!"

"William! William!"
"What in Merlin's beard is happening here?!" Catherine barges into Jasper's room and lunges onto his bead and starts to shake him by the shoulders. "Wake up, Jasper! Wake up! You're having a nightmare!"
Jasper finally awakens and tears start to run down his face. He grabs his mother and hugs her tightly. Confused and scared he starts to cry, and Catherine holds on to him tightly.
"There, there now, nothing to worry about, it was all in your head, nothing can hurt you here."
"Why did he leave, mother?!"
"Who?!"
"William."
Catherine looks around the room and sighs. "I love your brother deeply, and I miss him too. But you know what

happened that night. There was so much that did not make any sense at all. I was gutted when he left, absolutely devastated; we both were.

"I dreamt about him; I think he may be in some trouble."

"Merlin watches over all of us, don't worry. Now get some sleep because we have a big day ahead of us and we are taking those carrot cakes."

Jasper went back to sleep, and he needed to rest for, in a couple of hours, he would be on his way to Stonehenge to celebrate the summer solstice, the longest day of the year. A tradition that goes back all the way to the times of the druids and Merlin. A tradition now led by Socrates the owl and his covenant.

4 THE SUMMER SOLSTICE

ON THE 20ᵀᴴ OF JUNE, Jasper and Catherine woke up early in the morn to head towards Stonehenge, they had to be there latest by sunset to witness the ceremony. For a human, the distance would have been 14 to 15 hours on foot. With a horse and carriage going mildly fast it, would be one to two hours. Fortunately for the woodland creatures, their method of long-distance travel was different. They had an intricate and well-designed system of underground tunnels that allowed them to travel very quickly to some parts of the countryside. Some say that Merlin and his druids were the engineers of these tunnels, but, alas, we may never know.

Jasper started to gather all the cakes his mother had baked the night before; Jasper and Catherine, each, had their basket filled and with carrots. But before they left, Catherine had to make sure she was well presented for the ceremony, so she grabbed her light blue scarf and handbag. "Off we go, Jasper," said Catherine.

As they ventured deeper into the forest, the sun was rising, but Jasper was trying to stay awake and was having trouble paying attention where he was walking. Even though he was half-asleep, he was excited for the summer solstice at Stonehenge.

By noon, they came across a small hill and started to walk on it. There was nothing particularly interesting about this hill, but what was on the other side is something that many do not know about.

Once on the hill, they saw several piles of medium size rocks spread out from each other. They had to look for a specific pile that would lead them to an underground entrance.

Catherine walked down the hill in front of Jasper and walked towards to the rocks observing each one. "Mum, do you remember which pile?" asked Jasper as he yawned at the same time.

She asked Jasper to be silent as she was trying to remember which was the correct pile. "Aha, found it! Quickly come this way, Jasper," Catherine asks for Jasper's help to set aside the rocks. Mind you, some of the rocks were bigger than them.

Once cleared, there was a rather big hole in the ground.

"Alright, son, in you go."

"Cheers, mum."

Jasper made his way into the hole and, when he was deep enough, he could not see much. In fact it was very dark; Catherine was right behind him.

"This seems a little dodgy, mother; I can't see anything in here."

"Not to worry, it's part of the experience. Remember these tunnels were also made by the help of Merlin and his druids, so they are completely safe. Oh, fiddlesticks! Where is the flint to light this torch?"

"Mum?"

"Relax, it's here somewhere." Catherine continued to look for the flint and torch in her handbag.

"You forgot, didn't you?"

"Don't be acting smart with me, I always have plan. I know a bit of magic here and there, now hush."

Catherine placed her arms up high, and Jasper stood still hoping to survive for whatever may happen. She took a deep breath in.

"*Coram me Lux*!" said Catherine out loud. But nothing happened.

"That's it? Brilliant, mother."

"Wait a minute."

"We are wasting ti…"

"Shh! Hush, Jasper, look."

Out of nowhere hundreds and hundreds of small will-o-the-wisps had started to appear and started to elevate to the ceiling of the tunnel and Jasper was completely gobsmacked. The view was breathtaking; he never would have thought to see something so majestic in such a dark place.

"I never doubted you for a second mother."

"You were throwing a wobby."

"Was not; besides, who taught you that spell?"

"An old friend of mine; now come along or we will be late."

"Will you tell me who?"

"No, too long of a story, now come along, Jasper," said Catherine.

Jasper and Catherine followed the trail of will-o-the-wisps deeper into the tunnels. As they both walked guided by the atmospheric ghost lights, neither could deny how strikingly beautiful the view was. Jasper lifted his paw into the air to feel the warmth of his surroundings and the will-o-the-wisps danced gracefully.

It would be common to run into other animals in these tunnels, usually moles, for they prefer to live in dark places and in cold soil. They are not known for their hospitality; they can be very rude sometimes. It is preferably to be on your way if you encounter an angry mole. In other instances, they can be especially useful if you are extremely lost in these tunnels. Nevertheless, they are harmless creatures, they spend most of their time eating earthworms and insects. Especially larva's, give a mole a basket of larva's and he or she will befriend you most immediately.

"Jasper, Jasper! I think we're here; I can hear a lot of movement from above." Catherine was putting her ears on the walls of the tunnel and could feel a lot of vibration and noise coming from the top. "Quickly, we must dig up."

Jasper and Catherine started to dig up, they were making a new exit hole. Once the earth started to break from the inside, Catherine ears were popping from the ground as if she herself was a carrot, then Jasper's ears also popped out from the ground. Finally, both rabbits were able to break free from the tunnels and onto the surface. The moment they were on their legs, they could feel something approaching them. It was a horse hauling a wagon coming their way.

"Careful, Jasper, avoid the horse!" Both Catherine and Jasper jumps out of the way to avoid being run over.

"We were almost done for," said Jasper.

"Are the cakes all right?"

"A little tipped over, but they're fine."

"Well at least it's not a dog's dinner. Come along, I can see Stonehenge from where we are."

And there it was, the infamous stones where Merlin and the druids would gather and where the animals of Cirencester learned to speak the tongue of man. As they walked closer and closer to the elevated stones, more and more animals had started to appear. There must have been at least 2000 animals by the time they arrived: squirrels, possums, rabbits, birds, dear, foxes, badgers. And Jasper was so excited to see everyone gathering, he felt that he was becoming a part of history.

"Jasper! Jasper! Over here!" Jasper was being called out by someone, it sounded like Collin, but he could not see him through the crowd. "There you are, mate, can't see me, can't you. Look at this crowd, grand! Innit?"

"Yes, it's quite the crowd. I need to look where are we going to set up our tent; I have a cake and carrots in the basket."

"Lovely! Bagsy! Cheers, Jasper!" said Collin with much delight as he just grabbed a carrot from the basket without asking.

"Have you seen my mother?; I may have lost her when you called me," said Jasper.

"Oh! There she is, she's over there talking to some other rabbits," pointed out Collin.

"Great, I'm going to drop off these baskets with her so we can get closer to the Altar Stone."

They both walked past the Circle of the Sarsen Stones and Jasper was trying to figure out who was she speaking with.

"Mum, here are the basket of carrots Collin and …"

"Jasper sweetie, look who I found: Sarah and Eileen."

As Jasper laid the baskets onto the floor, he saw a rabbit that he has not seen in ages."

"Remember Sarah Taylor and her daughter Eileen Taylor?"

For one long moment, his breath was taken away and everything around him had started to slow down. He had seen beauty, but never like this. Eileen was a red rabbit with piercing green eyes; she wore a yellow scarf embroidered with small white flowers and had on a green dress. Her eyes were bright emerald, offering a window of peace and serenity. She radiated warmth and kindness, almost that of an angelic nature. Jasper just stood there dazzled, not saying much.

Catherine, gently elbowed Jasper and whispered to him in an unbelievably soft voice for him to say something. Collin noticed that this was very awkward.

"Collin Smith rabbit, a pleasure to make your acquaintance," said Collin as he lifted his top hat and extended his paw. "I believe Jasper is at a loss of words because yesterday we survived quiet the ordeal, and frankly it was traumatizing," continued Collin.

"Oh, my? May I ask what happened?" asked Sarah.

"Of course! You see, Jasper saved my life yesterday! A true hero he is, I broke into Old Crazy Maggie's house. Fortunately, Jasper's intellect got us out of there!" said Collin as he patted Jasper's shoulder. Catherine placed her paw over her face of the embarrassment she was going through.

"My goodness, how did you ever get out?" asked Sarah.

"That will be another tale for another moment, my dear Sarah, right, Jasper old boy?"

"Yes, somewhere along those lines," said Jasper nervously. "Forgive my silence, it has been a very long day," added Jasper apologetically.

"Oh! nothing to be sorry for, thank the stars the both of you lads are safe. We all know about Crazy Old Maggie, don't we, Eileen?" said Sarah.

"We've all heard the stories. Also, it's very nice to see you again, Jasper; it's been a long time since I last saw you, I think we were still in primary school," added Eileen.

"Well – I, yes, yes, it has been quite a while."

Catherine starts to clear her throat.

"Well, I think you three should wander around, and see what the other animals are up to, enjoy yourselves before the ceremony," said Catherine.

So, they did, Jasper was less nervous now. The three of them went to different tents, all the animals were giving out free food and ale, the event was full of rejoicing and exultation. Eileen and Jasper were getting along very quickly, and Collin was telling Eileen what they have been up to the last years. She really fascinated hearing all the different types of adventures Jasper and Collin were getting into.

Moments later all the animals that were in Stonehenge started to applaud and cheer as they could see the sun setting behind the horizon. They could also see Socrates the Owl and his flock of wise owls soaring in the sky. "Oh, let's stay here, Jasper, it's going to be impossible to get nearer to the Altar Stone at this point, its overly packed", said Eileen.

As the owls landed onto the Altar Stone, the roar of animals was higher than ever. The Covenant of Owls consisted of 12 members, Socrates being the lead told his right-hand owl Maximus to tell the others to form a circle so they could discuss the procedures of the ceremony.

Jasper was looking at Socrates as he was talking to the rest of the owls. He was a strict and a wise animal, but beneath the hard exterior was an animal who clearly cared about the other animals. Just by being in his presence he emitted energy and vitality. He brought a sense of calm amongst the other animals as well.

However, there were rumours that not everything was well; on that day, and for some years, Socrates has been worried about something. He tried awfully hard not to give away any concern. But I guess you can say it is a sixth sense of an animal to feel or perceive when something is wrong. But Jasper and the other animals never knew what it could be, so they never paid much attention to it.

The time was now 9 p.m. All the animals were silent, there were whispers here and there but nothing too loud. Around the stones, behind in front and even on top, all the animals stared at the Altar Stone waiting for Socrates to say something. The moment Socrates faced the animals the murmur of the crowd started to elevate.

"Fellow animals, happy solstice!" All the animals roared cheerfully in response. "We gather here today in this holy ground to honour our ancestors that were here before us and to the mystical druid Merlin that gave us the power of speech and knowledge that we have today!" The cheers intensify. "As some of you have heard, there is war amongst the humans; we have never been involved or affected by their actions of self-destruction, however the owls and I feel that is our duty to wish that this conflict ends and that we may never see any of it in our lands for the benefit of all animals and humans!"

The animals clapped in response.

"As it is tradition, I will commence the words that were said centuries before, and everyone here in unison must repeat what I say; now, we shall start facing the East." All the animals are silent once more and face the East. Socrates continues, "We call to the East and the powers of air, hail and welcome."

"Hail and welcome."

"May there be peace in the East."

"May there be peace in the East!"

"Inspire our thought and awaken our mind and the true power that lies in our thoughts, so mote it be."

"So mote it be!"

Socrates now commands the animals to turn to the South.

"We call the South in the power of fire, hail and welcome."

"Hail and welcome!"

"Ignite our passion and fire our hearts that we may stand with strength and courage in our true glory, so mote it be."

"So mote it be!"

"May there be peace in the South."

"May there be peace in the South!"

Socrates now commands the animals to turn to the West.

"We call to the West and the powers of water, Hail and Welcome."

"Hail and Welcome!"

"Go through our emotions and wash away our fears until we feel at peace with who we truly are, so mote it be."

"So mote it be!"

"May there be peace in the West."

"May there be peace in the West!"

Socrates now commands the animals to turn towards the North.

"We call the North and the powers of earth. Hail and Welcome."

"Hail and Welcome!"

"We honour our mother Earth, home to us all. May we strive to love and protect her. May there be peace in the North. So mote it be."

"So mote it be! May there be peace in the North!"

Socrates now calls upon all the animals present to face the middle of the Altar Stone, facing a basket of flowers and herbs.

"May there be peace in the world. So mote it be."

"May there be peace in the world! So mote it be!"

"Now, fellow animals, we will now invoke the power of the sun and of the earth. Starting with the sun, repeat after me.

"Great one of Heaven power of the Sun."

"Great one of Heaven power of the Sun!"

"Come again as a volt into our island."

"Come again as a volt into our island!"

"We call upon the ancients and the ones before us."

"We call upon the ancients and the ones before us!"

"Lift up my shining spear of light to protect us."

"Lift up my shining spear of light to protect us!"

"Put out the powers of darkness."

"Put out the powers of darkness!"

"Give us fair woodlands and green fields."

"Give us fair woodlands and green fields!"

"Blossoming orchards and ripening corn."

"Blossoming orchards and ripening corn!"

"And show us the lovely realm of the gods."
"And show us the lovely realm of the gods!"
"So mote it be."
"So mote it be!"

"Well done, fellow animals, now we shall evoke the power of the earth. Hypatia, if you would please." Socrates brings forth a female owl who is strong in the arts of incantations, mathematics, and astronomy.

"Repeat after me," said Hypatia as she approached the very edge of the Altar Stone with her wings spread out, looking upon the crowd.

"Oh, mighty mother of us all."
"Oh, mighty mother of us all!"
"Mother of all fruitfulness."
"Mother of all fruitfulness!"
"My flower and stem and barge and fruit."
"My flower and stem and barge and fruit!"
"My life, my love, and all growing things."
"My life, my love, and all growing things!"
"We call upon the earth, our lady of nature."
"We call upon the earth, our lady of nature!"
"Bring peace where there is strike."
"Bring peace where there is strike!"
"Bring love where there is hate."
"Bring love where there is hate!"
"And may all members of our animal family …"
"And may all members of our animal family …!"
"… Support and tolerate each other in a world without end."
"… Support and tolerate each other in a world without end!"
"So mote it be."
"So mote it be!"

"Finally, we will recite the hollow chant using three letters: 'I', that represents the Sun rising East, at the spring and autumn equinox. 'A' represents the Sun rising to the Northeast at summer solstice, southeast at the winter solstice, and 'O' is the earth going around the sun. Each letter represents a very important aspect of the universe, but especially the 'O' for it is the sound that resonates the most amongst the cosmos."

In that moment all the owls walked in the centre of the Altar Stone and lifted the basket of flowers and herbs; and in that very moment Socrates gave the signal with his wing for the animals to echo the three letters.

IIIIIIIIIIIIIIIIIIIIIIIIIIIIIIIIIIIIAAAAAAAAAAAAAAAAAAAAAAAAAAAAAAOOOOOOOOOOOOOOOOOOOO!

Echoed throughout Stonehenge, the more times the animals repeated these three letters, the sound and vibration was getting stronger. Shortly the sound would start to cause an effect on the stones: from their natural cold grey colour, slowly they were turning into a light blue shade, then into a bright piercing blue so bright that it could be seen kilometres away; it could outshine any star. The outer stones would then shoot a magnificent beam of blue light into the sky, sending all the good wishes and vibrations into the universe. And that would conclude the summer solstice ceremony.

"Happy solstice, everyone," cried Socrates. "Let us now celebrate."

In that moment all the animals were roaring with cheers and applauding that the ceremony went successful. All the rabbits, mice, badgers, foxes, birds were all happy and continued to pour the cider, lager and enjoy food they had brought. There were hundreds of tents and stands of every type of animals sharing and giving away bread with marmalade and honey, carrots, biscuits, tea, roasted potatoes; it was a never-ending feast.

"I reckon that was some spectacle, wouldn't you say?" asked Eileen to Jasper.

"Indeed, it was, now we just have to enjoy what's left; it looks like Mr. Possum over there is going to go through a bender." Both just laughed as Jasper was pointing out that Mr. Kevin Possum was going through his 8th pint of cider as if there was not enough for everybody.

"I need to get back with my mother, Jasper; it was nice seeing you again, I hope to catch up soon."

"Of course," replied Jasper as he watched Eileen go into the crowd.

Collin popped out of nowhere snickering. "Guess who owes me a favour, huh? I saved you back there, old bean," said Collin laughing.

The rest of the evening became one giant celebration, and the animals could enjoy their time outside of the forest uninterrupted till sunrise. Until the premonition.

5 THE OMEN

AROUND 6 IN THE MORN, most of the animals were half asleep after much eating and drinking. A few were awake watching the calming sunrise. Collin, on the other hand was completely passed out in a barrel with his top hat covering his face for he had too many rounds and was well rested.

Catherine and Sarah were awake, cleaning up the food they had brought to Stonehenge, and Jasper and Eileen were on a hill, not too far from the rest of the animals, where they too were observing the sunrise. Both Eileen and Jasper were drinking a pint of cider as they were retelling each of their own shares of stories and adventures.

"Jasper, what you think lies beyond Gloucestershire and Wiltshire?" asked Eileen as she took a gulp of cider.

"My brother William asked himself that same question years ago, and off he went to London, out of the blue. Haven't heard from him ever since," replied Jasper has he too drank from his pint.

"I'm sorry to hear that."

"No worries, it's all right. Hey, by the way, did you notice the owls were all night talking amongst themselves as if something was wrong? Socrates knows something that we don't," said Jasper.

"Yes, I noticed that too. I wonder what it could be. Anyways, Jasper, as much as I am enjoying seeing the sunrise with you, which I really am, I am also absolutely knackered and off to Bedfordshire."

"Off to where?"

"I said I'm really tired and I am off to bed silly," said Eileen laughing.

"I'm knackered too, I'm going to help my mother tiding up," said Jasper.

"Let me help you before I go home," replied Eileen.

Jasper and Eileen went running into the crowd of hungover animals. Some of them could not even stand correctly. It was quite funny to watch. Jasper knew that many of them were going to have a horrendous headache in a couple of more hours.

As the sun continued to rise, more and more animals were starting to awaken including the owls. They were having trouble locating their kin, so they went towards the stones to see if they were there. When Jasper and Eileen got near Stonehenge, there was something crackling in front of the altar stone, it was the bonfire that was lit last night. Jasper and Eileen just stood there from a distance observing it. Jasper felt the need to approach it, so he did.

"Jasper, what are you doing? Come back!" said Eileen in a loud whisper while trying not to awake the other sleeping animals.

"It's fine don't worry, stay back," said Jasper.

Jasper continued to approach the bonfire, he could clearly see the wood was all burnt, and that there was no fire, so where was this crackling coming from?

Socrates was starting to awaken, he and the other owls were sleeping near to the Altar Stone. When he woke up, he could see Jasper approaching the crackling bonfire, and the more he approached the more crackling there was. Jasper kept walking towards it as if he was in a sort of trance. Socrates quickly jumped from the stone and grabbed Jasper before he got nearer to the ferocious crackling from the bonfire. Socrates wrapped Jasper in his wings, and they both crashed landed onto the ground. Jasper hits his head against the floor and breaks from the trance.

Socrates alerts the other owls of the fire and now they can see the crackling intensifying. Socrates tells Jasper to close his eyes and turn away. All of the sudden there is a bright white light shooting up from the bonfire straight towards the sky that followed with the sound of an explosion. But it was not a pleasant light, it was not a warm light, it was a light so bright that it was painful to watch. By now all the animals that were asleep around Stonehenge were awaken by the light. As the light started to dim the animals started to look at it, including Jasper and Socrates.

The light beam that was pointed towards the sky had started to widen itself. And disturbing imagery would start to appear, images that would haunt every single animal that was present. Jasper gazed very closely to the light and could not redirect his sight. From within the beam they all saw their beautiful green hills of the countryside turned to ash with enormous holes all over the land.

There were no longer be green trees but burnt twigs, the rivers and streams would be dried up and only remain the withered bodies of fish. Cirencester and the other villages in the Cotswold would be on fire, buildings collapsing, houses torn apart, blocks of stone on the streets, as well of the bodies of humans. Then they all saw a large city. Fire and lighting would rain from above destroying everything that it touched. There would be chaos on the streets, humans looking for refuge and all that could be seen were those gigantic iron eagles that Jasper had seen in his dreams. Those very same monstrosities would be flying over the city annihilating everyone and everything. And behind that city was a falcon, with a scar on his right eye, dressed in gold and fire.

The light finally grew bigger, gave a final aggressive white flash, and disappeared along with the images that everyone could feel and see.

"May Merlin watch on all of us," whispered Socrates.

Silence echoed through the early morning at Stonehenge. No one could really comprehend what had just happened. Socrates and the other owls gathered onto the Altar Stone to discuss the nature of the premonition and what should be done. The other animals had started to talk silently amongst themselves; nobody wanted to jump into conclusions or yell something to not cause a panic amongst the crowd. Even though all were now afraid, and the young ones were holding tightly to their parents, everyone wanted an answer. Socrates turned around towards the animals.

"Animals, please remain calm!" said Socrates with an elevated voice. The animals start to murmur amongst themselves. "This is a very rare phenomenon during the summer solstice!"

"What does this mean, Socrates?!" asked one animal from the crowd.

Socrates takes a deep breath. "It means we need to prepare for the worst. Troubled times are upon us."

"What do you mean for the worst?!"

"When will this happen?!"

"Was that Alistair, Socrates?!" That question haunted him, and Jasper could see it in his face.

"Indeed, that was Alistair the falcon, some of you may not know who he is, but he is not of a pure soul, but an evil soul and it seems that he is back."

Socrates was again bombarded with questions regarding Alistair, if whether they were safe or not. Panic was starting to arise amongst the animals.

"Order! We need order!" cried Socrates. "We do not know when the omen will occur!" But the older animals continued to ask about Alistair. The only thing Socrates told the animals was that they mustn't worry about him. Some of the animals were already starting to pack up their belongings and head back home. Eileen walked towards Jasper where he was left by Socrates.

"It's not safe here, we must leave," said Eileen.

"Let's go," replied Jasper.

In the middle of a panic, with the animals running chaotically, Jasper was holding Eileen's paw and looking for their tent. When they found it, Collin was still trying to wake up from last night, but Catherine and Sarah were already packing their things.

"Jasper we need to await Socrates instructions before we leave," said Catherine.

"Animals of the forest, you must listen to me! Whatever may come we will endure, and we will survive! The owls and I have protected you before, we have banished evil from this place, and we will continue to do so as long as we are here!" The animals cheered in response. But deep down inside, Socrates was worried of what was to come.

6 UNEASINESS AT HOME

TWO MONTHS HAD PASSED by since the summer solstice and it was August 21st, 1940. During the last 60 days the animals of the forest were not light-hearted, and tensions were rising amongst themselves.

Bigger animals were acting more aggressive and started stealing food rations from smaller ones, hoarding food, not sharing with others, in fear of what may happen. Friendships that had lasted for years had turned into animosities, joyous days of bathing under the sun had turned into grey and rainy days waiting for the worst to come and not knowing when.

Everyone was living in paranoia, trying to protect their families from the worst-case scenarios. The owls would regularly fly from Oxford to the forest to try to calm the animals, breaking up the fights seemed unsuccessful as the fighting became more frequent.

Many small birds that resided in the forest had flown away, the moles were deep underground, and the squirrels, rabbits, possums, badgers, and mice that remained were deep in their huts and holes.

It was three rabbits that maintained their calm, that avoided trouble with other animals, they still had that sense of community within them, to stand their ground and not sulk in fear.

Jasper was in the northern part of the forest helping Collin dig an underground hut where he could hide his food from being stolen.

"No human war or some falcon named Alistair will make me abandon my abode; load of rubbish this is, if you ask me," said Collin as he and Jasper were walking out from the hut to take break from the digging.

"No one is making you leave your home, Collin, just relax a bit."

"Take a gander, Jasper, almost all the animals are gone, and the few ones that are left are raiding other homes for food! I will not run and hide from no one!"

"Besides, who is this Alistair fellow? Never have I heard of him. Some of the other animals keep talking about him, and when I ask about him, I get no answers," said Collin.

"I'm with you there, no idea, but something to do with the forest though; a lot of the animals are shaken up by that falcon," replied Jasper.

"Hullo there, boys!" Collin quickly jumped holding on to his top hat and stood behind Jasper holding tight to his shovel. As he looked over Jasper's shoulder, he saw that it was Eileen approaching them.

"Collin, the whole bloody forest can hear your nonsense, no one is coming for your tobacco or carrots," said Eileen amusingly.

"And what may you be doing here if I may inquire, you ginger hare?" responded Collin with a stuck-up attitude.

"Easy, Collin, that is no way to treat a guest, be nice," said Jasper.

"Thank you, Jasper, I happen to be here around these parts because I've heard rumours of an unusual gathering of humans occurring at this moment in the town square," said Eileen.

"Unusual, you say? How unusual?" asked Collin.

"Well, I was actually thinking of going myself to see what the fuss is all about," responded Eileen.

"You're saying your off to Cirencester, by yourself? When there are probably more humans? Your mad," said Collin.

"Are you saying that Collin Smith is afraid? Ha! I though you loved a good adventure, how about you, Jasper? Are you keen in coming with me?" asked Eileen.

"Gladly, something to get my mind of this war and falcon nonsense," responded Jasper.

"Hold on! Hold on! Don't be daft, I ain't afraid of anything. Besides, I can't let this one go off by himself. He needs me!" Collin stops what he is doing, grabs his top hat, sticks his pipe in his mouth, pats himself down and starts walking downhill. "Well, aren't you both coming?"

Jasper and Eileen laughed at how easily it is to provoke Collin.

"Oh, be quiet you two," said Collin.

"Oi! Collin, more of that attitude and your mush will be meeting my paw very soon," said Eileen.

"Thanks for the warning, darling", replied Collin.

And they all laughed as they headed towards Cirencester.

7 BACK TO CIRENCESTER

JASPER, COLLIN, AND EILEEN, three rabbits, a grey, black and a red one stood at the gate of Cirencester. It was mid-day, and the weather was fair. This time they were not going to get carrots; the objective was quite simple, go into town, get near the parish and see what all the commotion is about.

Fortunately, the parish was not far from the entrance to the forest. The rabbits ran rapidly down the pavement under the cover of the trees and bushes to hide themselves from the sight of humans. As they ran down Coxwell Street they noticed that there weren't that many humans to be seen wandering around.

When they reached the end of Coxwell Street, they took a right on Gosditch Street and the parish would be all the way straight forward. However, before they could even make it halfway towards the street, the area was filled with humans wearing uniforms; they wore a brown–khaki colour clothing from head to toe and they were holding their rifles.

The three of them knew that it would be too risky and dangerous wandering amongst the crowd, so they had to come up with a plan. In front of the parish stood a single man in uniform addressing the other humans, but it was difficult to hear from the distance, so they had to get closer.

Jasper pointed out to the group that if they could hop on the ledge of the wall, walk straight towards the side entrance, enter the church, maybe they could hear what the soldier was saying.

In a straight-line Jasper, Collin and Eileen ran straight towards the side entrance of the church undetected by the large crowd of humans that was growing by the minute. When the three of them arrived at the door they saw that it was slightly open, so they entered. Once inside they closed the door behind them. They all took deep breaths in and were happy that no one saw them. The three rabbits slowly walked in and hopped onto the benches of the church and started to look around, gazing at the detailed architecture that was there, the columns with arches and the wooden ceiling were a geometrical delight for the sight.

"It's my first time in here," said Collin.

"Same for me," replied Eileen.

"I think it's the first time for everyone in here," added Jasper.

The three of them observed the different coloured stained glass high up on the walls, the patterned floor, the texture of the stone columns and then finally the altar.

Collin was very curious about learning human traditions, but he never had the opportunity to observe their religious customs. As he approached the altar there were certain imagery of humans that made him think of Merlin. There were four images of four humans in stained glass. They were wearing crowns and had staffs. Above them it seemed to be images of other humans, but they looked to be of less importance because their size was smaller.

"I don't know but I'm thinking these four humans in front of me, might be the human's version of Merlin," noted Collin.

"Maybe, remember that Merlin himself was a human," said Jasper.

"Boys! Boys! Over here I found a way to get up to the very top; come on!" cried Eileen.

Jasper and Collin decided that they would philosophize on human religious beliefs some other day. They now ran towards Eileen to see that she had stumbled upon a secret passageway within the stone walls that led up to the second floor. The three of them went running as fast as they could so anxious in seeing a better view of the town square. Through several twists and turns they reached to a level that was sealed shut with a wooden door.

"Come on, lads, help me open the door! Heave! Heave!" said Eileen. The three rabbits with all there might managed to open the door by accidentally breaking it. To their surprise they had stumbled upon a family of mice that were in a state of repose.

"Oh, look how exciting it seems that we have some visitors," said one of the mice that was serving tea to her children.

"Awfully sorry to intrude like this, we were unaware there were mice living here, we wanted to reach the highest point," said Jasper.

"Please do come in, no need to apologize, that door was going to be taken down either way. We're just having a cuppa tea; would you fancy one yourselves?" asked the father mice as he was smoking from a pipe and wearing a plaid tweed waistcoat.

With some hesitation the rabbits kindly accepted the offer. "That sounds splendid, thank you very much, this is a true delectation," replied Eileen in a very politely fashion.

"Allow us to introduce ourselves, my name is Jasper, and these are my companions Collin and Eileen."

"How lovely, my name is Janice Baker, this is my husband Harold Baker and the three young ones you see here are Henry, Samantha and Ethan." The three young mice just smiled and waved back politely as they were having their tea and jam sandwiches. "Pleasure; we are really awfully sorry about the door though," said Eileen.

"Oh please don't feel bad my dear girl, that door was to keep the cat out, he's been gone for ages, never could get us, suppose he just left ha!" said Janice.

"Would you mind if I join you in a smoke Mr. Baker?" asked Collin.

"By all means, please do, not many animals accompany me with the tobacco smoking these days, being in the middle of Cirencester and all. Where did you rabbits say you were from?

"We come from the forest," replied Collin.

"Ah, yes the forest, we haven't been over there in quite sometime," said Harold reminiscing on how he would spend his youth running around the trees. "Rather good times if I say so, indeed," said Harold as he kept smoking from his pipe.

"If you don't mind me asking, how is it that you and your family are here?" asked Jasper.

"Well, you see, Harold and I used to live in the forest like yourselves many years ago. And, one day, we accidentally bumped into each other in the town square to find some food and take back to forest for our families, mind you we didn't know each other in that moment," said Janice as she looked at her three mice drinking their tea and listening.

"Oh, darling don't give them the long version." chuckled Harold. "You see, there was a predicament," said Harold.

"What was that predicament?" asked Eileen.

"Cheese," said both Harold and Janice. "Well, we ended up fighting for the same piece of cheese, it was a proper brawl if you will. After the struggle I felt so bad, that I shared my cheese with him, you know, no hard feelings.

And as time flew by, we started to come into town together for more cheese and then, we came into town as our own little escape for dates and, well, we fell in love and decided to make this centre of worship our new home," said Janice.

"How romantic!" said Eileen with plenty of enthusiasm.

"Quite so, my dear, and what brings you to Cirencester, may I ask?" asked Harold.

"Ask away, Harold, for you have been such a generous host." Harold just chuckles to the compliment Collin gave him.

"We heard there was an unusual gathering of humans here and we wanted to see what it was about. You see, things haven't been going so well in the forest. This past summer solstice, there was a bitter omen, about the human war that's happening, and the name Alistair the falcon was mentioned," said Jasper.

You could hear the teacup hitting the saucer the moment they heard the name Alistair. The rabbits noticed this.

"Are ... are you alright Janice?" asked Eileen. Both Janice and Harold had very serious facial expressions. Janice even told her children to go into their rooms and close the door.

"After all these years, I never thought I would have to hear that name again," said Janice.

"Is something wrong? We apologize if we caused any upset," said Jasper.

"Not your fault, my boy, not your fault," said Harold as he continued to smoke his pipe. "We have heard rumours of the human conflict intensifying, but Alistair returning is...another story," added Harold.

"Who is he? And why won't the other animals tell us who he is?" asked Collin.

"When we were younger, Alistair was a vicious, vile, evil, horrible, horrible falcon that caused a myriad of suffering in the village before you three were born. You have no idea how dark and ghastly living in the forest was back in those days. I would assume the others would rather forget he even existed, for that reason they avoid telling you who he is," said Harold.

"What happened?" asked Jasper.

Janice clears her throat. "Well...I don't know the whole story, but, when Alistair was young, he was a student, trained by Socrates, he was his protégé in one way or another. Rumour has it that at some point he became power hungry and started to learn forbidden magic. He stayed amongst the animals and slowly started to corrupt the minds of the others, he defiled the owls, and the teachings of the druids. He convinced other animals to act more savagely, more primal amongst each other. He had a goal, but no one knew what it was. Things became dreadful in the forest, horrendous, that was until Socrates took care of him, at least we thought he did. Indeed, it was dark times in Cirencester," said Janice.

"My mum wouldn't tell me all this," said Jasper.

"It's understandable, my dear. And who may your mother be if, I may ask?" said Janice.

"Catherine Jones," replied Jasper.

"Wait, Catherine Jones? Catherine Jones the rabbit?" asked Janice.

"Why? Do you know her?" replied Jasper.

"Know her? She saved my father from kicking the bucket! Oh! Blessed be my stars! The son of Catherine in my house! This is truly a blessing!" said Janice as tears ran down her face. She walked over to Jasper and gave him a big hug."

"Let's not speak of that foul bird, I'm sure whatever the omen is, Socrates and the owls will get on it right away." added Janice.

"Wait a minute, how exactly do you know my mother? And what do you mean she help you save your father? I'm unaware of this."

"Jasper, you must forgive me, but I cannot say no more, we took an oath to not mention this story. I'm sorry but it will be something you will have to ask your mother," said Janice.

"How about we distract ourselves by seeing what's all the fuss outside our home, eh?" suggested Harold.

In the room they were in, there was an opening in the wall that allowed them to see and hear what was going outside. High above, they saw that there were more humans than before and they could hear what the uniformed human in the middle of the square was saying.

"Now", he said peremptorily, "step forward, please. One at a time, and no shoving. One at a time with no shoving."

"Sir, are we being invaded?!"

"Are we safe here in Cirencester?!"

"What are we to do with the young ones and elderly?!"

"What is going to happen to our homes?!"

The crowd had started to swarm the soldier with questions.

"As you know, we are at war with Germany, we are going to evacuate the children and elderly in different parts of the countryside. If air raids start it will be the bigger cities that will be targeted. People who will remain in Cirencester must take shelter in the bunkers."

"Hun, do you think we'll be safe here?" asked Janice with a bit of worry.

"I'd say so my dear, who would want to destroy our lovely home, we pose no threat to no one," affirmed Harold.

When Jasper heard the soldier mention that bigger cities may be targeted, he was thinking again of his brother William and of his dream. As he continued to hear all the arguing and questioning being done amongst the humans,

Jasper noticed that they were behaving very similar to the animals of the forest in times of panic.

"Harold and Janice, thank you so much for the hospitality, but we must be on our way. I think we have heard enough for today from the humans. We should tell the animals what we saw today," said Jasper.

"Of course, my lad, no worries. Here, take some of this cheese, it's very delicious, it has a smoky flavour to it," said Harold as he handed it to Collin. Collin opened his satchel, placed the cheese in and raised his top hat in gratitude. Eileen was getting up from the table as well and thanked Janice for the tea, cheese and jam sandwiches.

"Jasper, here, take this." Janice was opening her purse and gave him a transparent flask that contained a glowing light blue liquid. "This liquid is magical, it was given to me by a druid. Oh, my stars, how I cherish that day, Merlin is good to us all. Show this to your mother, she will know what it is," said Janice with a big smile.

"I will, thank you," replied Jasper.

"And forgive me about going on about Alistair, we meant not to frighten you three," added Janice.

"It will take a lot more than a bird the scare us three," said Jasper with a smile.

Everyone said their goodbyes and the rabbits were invited by the mice to come and drop by whenever they wanted. The rabbits made their way downstairs.

"What do we do now?" asked Collin.

"I reckon we should head back home and tell the others what we heard," said Eileen. And off to Cirencester they went.

8 DISTRESS IN THE FOREST

BY THE TIME JASPER, Eileen and Collin arrived at their hidden village in the forest, they could see that Socrates and the other owls were spread out, flying over what seemed to be an unorganized gathering of the animals. There was some sort of commotion happening, and they could also see that there were several of them cramped up into one area.

"Where are my turnips, you bloody thief?!" said one badger.

"Never trust a badger, backstabbing foul creatures!" replied one rabbit.

"The whole lot of you can rot!"

"STOP IT! STOP IT! screamed Socrates trying to break up the animals.

Socrates and his owls were doing their best to keep the other animal's calm. Jasper saw that his mother was in the crowd, but she was not in the mob fighting with the other animals. She was kneeled on the ground trying to help Eileen's mother, Sarah. Jasper and the rest quickly ran to see what was wrong with Sarah.

"Mummy! Mummy! What happened?! Are you all right?!"

"Eileen, my dear! I need you to step back a bit, your mother was attacked!"

Jasper and Collin did not know what to do, all they could see was Catherine was putting pressure onto Sarah's head as her paws were slowly getting covered in blood while the chaos was growing around them.

"Bloody hell, she is not responding, boys!" Jasper and Collin are immobilized.

"BOYS! Eyes here! Look at me! I need you to help me carry Sarah back to my house, only there is where I can help her, not in the middle of this mess!"

Eileen was in tears, wanting her mother to respond, but there was no movement.

"Ok, lads, grab her by the legs, one on each side and I'll grab her by the shoulders! Eileen, I need you to focus with me, dear, YES?! You are scared, I know, so am I, but right now we need to help your mother, help me to help her! Now grab her shoulder!"

Eileen wiped her tears off and helped Catherine. Slowly but steadily, they started to move away from the crowd.

"C'mon we are nearly there! Hurry!"

As they all walked away from the fight, Eileen kept on calling her mother to see if she would wake up.

"Mother, please wake up!"

There was still no response. It took them about 15 minutes of walking to get to Catherine's home. You could still hear the fighting and the arguing in the distance. When the rabbits finally arrived at the house, they quickly went inside. The house smelled of gingerbread and orange peel.

"Quickly! Put her on my bed, we cannot waste any time! Hurry!"

They were now walking towards Catherine's room panting and sweating, walking pass the living room without a care, knocking everything that stood in their way. Once inside Catherine's room they carefully placed her on the bed, and she was still not reacting. Catherine took charge of the situation.

"Jasper, I need you to boil hot water now!"

"Collin, I need you to go into the living room and look in the white drawer cabinet and bring me all of the bandages you can find."

"Eileen, go into the kitchen and lay on the table all of the medical herbs you can find, there should be calendula, lady's mantle, stinging nettle and evening primrose!"

Everyone scattered out of the room to tend to their individual duties. When the three young rabbits where out of the room, Catherine saw that the impact that Sarah had on her head was more severe than what she thought. The bleeding continued.

"Here you go, Catherine, here are the bandages!"

"Thank you, Collin! Go with Jasper and see if he needs help."

"Merlin, be merciful; Sarah, you must wake up, do it for your daughter."

Jasper barges in back into the room.

"Mum, the water is boiling, now what?!"

Catherine wiped a small tear from her eye and took a deep breath. Jasper stands for a moment in the entrance of the room trying to remember when was the last he had seen her mother tear up. She always tried to show strength in front of her son, she never liked to be seen crying or show any sign of vulnerability, but everyone was vulnerable that night.

"'Tell Eileen to put the herbs into the pot of boiling water."

Jasper and Collin stormed into the kitchen to see Eileen shaking.

"Bloody herbs! Which is which?!" said Eileen.

Collin slowly approaches Eileen from the back and gently places his paws on her shoulders.

"Eileen ... step aside, let Jasper look which ones your mother needs, yeah?"

As they both stepped aside Jasper walk towards the table to see what's in front of him.

"Ok, let's sort this out, here is the calendula ... lady's mantle ... stinging nettle."

Jasper was trying very hard not to get the herbs mixed up.

"Aha! Found it! Evening primrose! Quickly, the water is already boiling; we need to put it into the cauldron!"

Jasper placed all the herbs needed into the cauldron and with a large wooden spoon he swirled all of the ingredients in the boiling water. Unexcitingly, there was a chemical reaction from the plants: the cauldron had started to tremble and loads of foam had started overflowing the cauldron and pouring onto the floor. Not knowing what is happening, the three rabbits slowly retracts backwards.

"Jasper, what is happening?" asked Eileen.

"I'm not sure but we should stay away," replied Jasper.

"Since when does your mother know magic potions?" asked Collin.

"I found out myself not too long ago she has some family secrets I have never heard of," said Jasper.

When the foam ceased to spread, the three of them approached the cauldron to see what was in it. It looked like tea; the smell was delightful and had a strong earthy presence.

"JASPER! I NEED THAT HOT WATER WITH HERBS NOW!" shouted Catherine.

"Quick! Collin hand me a mug!" said Jasper.

Collin goes to one of the cupboards and tosses Jasper a porcelain mug. Jasper starts to slowly to pour the tea into the mug and runs toward his mother.

"Here is the tea, mum!"

Jasper, Collin and Eileen all stand near the door. Jasper is starting to sweat and leaves his coat on a chair in a corner of the room.

"You three, I need you to leave this room, I need to do something."

"What are you going to do to my mother?" asked Eileen.

"All will be well, dear. I need the three of you to trust me and pray to Merlin, but I need privacy. Now, go!"

"Please help my mum, Catherine, I'm begging you!" said Eileen right before Catherine closed the door.

The three rabbits that came with much enthusiasm from Cirencester were gathered in the living room wondering what was going to happen. There was total silence and each one was looking at each other for answers. Eileen was the rabbit that was worried the most.

"I need to know who did this to my mother! I need to know!" Eileen was clenching her paws, both Jasper and Collin could see that she went from sad and worried to mad and vengeful.

"Sarah will make it through, right now there is nothing we can do," said Jasper trying to calm her down.

"I think I will get some fresh air; I'll smoke my pipe outside to calm the nerves," added Collin.

"Go ahead, will be there in a moment," replied Jasper.

"It hurts Jasper, it hurts a lot to see her like this. My mother is good rabbit, she would never do anything to harm another animal!

"We will go to the owls and get to the bottom of this. Socrates will know what to do. Right now, we need to stay calm. I'm not sure what my mum is doing in there, but she's doing something! You saw what happened in the kitchen with the herbs! My mum knows magic!"

"Jasper … Eileen, I think you two need to come out and see this," said Collin.

Jasper and Eileen looked at each other in wonder; judging by the tone of Collin's voice, something seemed a little off. They were walking towards to the front door of the house, and as soon as they opened it, they saw a multitude of animals outside Jasper's house, and each one was holding a lit candle. It was a sight to see, hundreds of animals with lit candles standing next to each other, some of the animals had started to tear up. Whole families were there, even the ones that were gnawing and fighting against each other.

"What in the world...?"

Collin was smoking from his pipe and making smoke rings and as he observed the spectacle.

"There are still things in this here forest that will somehow always amaze me," said Collin.

Meanwhile, back in Catherine's room, she was trying to have Sarah drink the tea. She was half awake and in pain, she couldn't even open her mouth or her eyes and was only able to take little sips of the tea. Catherine had started to rub her paws together to warm them up through friction and place them over cheeks and forehead.

"C'mon, Sarah, don't you go out on me now; I've seen you get through harder things." Sarah was not responding to anything Catherine was doing or saying.

She observed Sarah's breath was decreasing, getting shorter and shorter. Catherine again tried to make her drink the tea, but it was no use.

Catherine set aside the mug on the nightstand next to her, and she slowly got up thinking what else she could do. She walked around the room thinking and thinking on how to save her; she sat on the chair that was on in the corner of the room. She accidentally sat over Jasper's coat. She felt an odd object. Catherine got up and saw that there was a very low glow emitting from the pocket and it caught her eyes. Catherine knew better not to meddle in other people's belongings, but she was magically drawn to it. Catherine placed her paw into the jacket and could touch the object, it was cold, cold as ice and pulled it out.

Before her was the transparent flask that Janice the mouse gave to Jasper. Catherine looked at the low blue glow that radiated from the flask; in that moment, she knew what it was. She knew what she had to do.

"Where is Socrates?! Where is he?! I want to speak with him!" cried Eileen.

From the sky, Socrates flew to the scene; he landed without making much noise, he stood in front of the three rabbits. Eileen still had tears in her eyes, but she was very mad.

"Socrates!" Her voice is starting to break. "Can you please tell me why my mother was attacked? Who did this?!

Socrates stood there listening to Eileen. He looked around staring at the animals that were holding the candles. He turned his head back and looked in the crowd and nodded. From the mass of animals that were there, came out a limping weasel that was hurt.

"Sweet child, before you is the one that attacked your mother, I will let you decide his fate. But before you choose you will listen to what he has to say," said Socrates.

All eyes were on Eileen, there were low whispers from the crowd as the animals discussed amongst themselves what fate would the weasel have. Eileen's paws were crunching with anger, her breath was long and hot, and her eyes were filled with fury. Eileen looked down on the weasel; she actually recognized the weasel, his name was James. James was hurt, not by the owls, but by the other animals in the brawl that was occurring earlier that day. He had a black eye and by the look of several intents of trying to stand up, his left leg was broken.

"Why did you attack my mother, James?" asked Eileen in an assertive tone.

"I—"

"Speak up, James!"

"Forgive me, it was not my intention to do her harm. My children they ... they are hungry, and so is my wife.

The other animals and I included are having trouble to find food. Everything about the human war and Alistair is making everyone uneasy!" The mention of 'Alistair' incremented the whispers amongst the animals.

"That gives you no reason to do what you did! NO REASON AT ALL! I don't care about no war or bloody bird! What you did was wrong!"

"I know, Eileen, your mother and a couple other animals were carrying food in the forest and—"

"And what, JAMES?! You all jumped her?! You all attacked her?! A defenseless mother?!"

"I am sorry, forgive me—" James lowered his head and stared at the floor in sadness, his nails were clawing through the soil of the ground as his guilt and fault was slowly consuming him from the inside.

"If it was food all that you wanted my mother would have shared it with you, you damn fool!"

"I was being selfish, I was hungry, my boys are hungry."

"I may never forgive you for what you did, but I know my mother would have. Socrates, let him go. I wish no harm to be set on James."

Socrates nodded with the other owls that were present. James tried to get up but kept falling back onto the ground. From the crowd came his two sons trying to help their father stand up. They were a bit younger than Jasper and Collin; one of them made eye contact with Eileen, they both stared into each other's eye, the whole situation to them both seemed so surreal.

"Thank you, Eileen," said James and she did not respond back. One of the young weasels turned his head and lifted his paw as a sign of gesture for letting his father go. Eileen did the same and watched the weasels walk back into the crowd. Eileen now slightly trembling quickly walked back towards the house to check in on her mother without saying anything to anyone. But before she could go any further Socrates called her name.

"Eileen, do you know why I let you choose the fate of James?"

"No, I need to see my mother!"

Socrates flew and landed on the roof of Jaspers house and directed himself to all the animals present.

"Animals of the forest, for the last past three months you have attacked your friends, brothers and sisters all between yourselves. Do you not see that the enemy is not your fellow animal? The enemy is fear and you have allowed it to grow amongst yourselves. You have allowed fear to give you reasons to argue and fight against each other. We were blessed with the gift of speech and intelligence to live with each other, not fight. The only animal here, that has shown mercy is Eileen. If one animal can show mercy, why can't you? For generations we have learned to coexist, we must end these senseless quarrels," said Socrates.

All the animals had started to talk amongst themselves and were looking at each other; soon all the animals that were arguing where starting to apologize to each other and ask forgiveness for their past aggressions.

"Why did you let me choose the faith of the weasel?" asked Eileen to Socrates.

"I have known you since you were a young rabbit, you have always shown compassion and care for others, and I knew you would do the same in this situation. The other animals needed to see that kindness. It is something that we all have and is something that we must practice daily."

"Thank you, Socrates, but what about the rest of the animals, why are they here?"

"Sweet Eileen, the animals are here praying to Merlin that your mother gets better. Jasper's mother is the few rabbits that I know off that can help her. She also has some knowledge of the druids. She's going to be ok!"

Catherine came out of the hut looking as she hasn't slept for days.

"Collin, give me that pipe." Catherine snatched the Collin's pipe before he could react. She was so tired that she sat on a small boulder that was in the front garden and took a couple of puffs. All the animals were shocked.

"Eileen, you mum will be fine, dear."

"That is wonderful news, Catherine , how did you do it?" asked Socrates.

Catherine took a deep breath and exhale, and gave the pipe back to Collin.

"Well, it seems these three here had a little something that came handy in the last minute." Jasper, Collin and Eileen were silent for they did not know what Catherine was talking about.

"That transparent flask that you had in your jacket Jasper, well that's what saved her. Do either of you fancy a cup of tea? Merlin knows I need one."

"I'm quite alright thank you, Catherine," replied Socrates in a very polite manner.

"I don't think I follow here," said Eileen.

"Quite simple, dear, would like a cuppa of tea, yay or nay? Your mother will be fine, but we need to discuss the flask".

"Yay please," said Jasper confusingly.

"Lovely, Jasper, Collin, Socrates, please stay, the rest of you lot, I thank you for beautiful vigil and all the support for Sarah, but it is time you all go back home. Oh! And I'm sure from now on forward we will all stop this childish squabble amongst us," said Catherine to all the animals that were around her house.

As Catherine went back into her house to get her cup of tea, the rest of the animals retreated back to their respective homes without noise. But the energetic atmosphere was uplifting.

Collin approaches Jasper. "I'm with Eileen, old chap, I'm not sure I'm following everything that is happening."

Jasper looked at both Eileen and Collin, and their facial expressions were the same as his; no one knew what Catherine was talking about, the only thing they knew was that Sarah was going to be well and there will be tea.

"Socrates, do you know what my mum is talking about?" asked Eileen.

"I may have an idea; did you happen to run into someone new in Cirencester?" replied Socrates.

"We met a lovely family of mice, Janice and Harold," replied Collin.

"Then, yes, I may have an idea what Catherine is on about."

Moments later, Catherine came out with a tray that had a kettle and teacups. She walked towards Eileen, gave her a hug and a cup of tea.

"Jasper, Collin, you boys can serve yourselves," said Catherine.

"Catherine, as much as I am grateful for saving my mother, I am awfully confused, none of us had any medicine, the only thing we brought back from Cirencester was a flask given to Jasper from a family of mice," said Eileen.

"Could it have been from a family of mice where husband and wife be Harold and Janice?" asked Catherine.

"Why yes! She mentioned you helped her father," said Eileen.

"That be true. Now, Jasper, what else did she mention regarding the flask?" asked Catherine to Jasper.

"Well, not much, she just mentioned that I should show it to you, that you would now what it is.

"Socrates, this is what I found in my son's Jacket." Catherine extended her hand and showed Socrates the transparent flask with glowing liquid. He grabs the flask with his wing and brings it up closer to his face so he can have a better look at it. As the blue glare reflected upon his face his eyes widened up.

"Eileen, you should consider yourself and your mother to be very lucky."

"What does luck have to do with anything happening here?"

"That blue shining liquid is called Elixir of Revival. In fact, it was given to us by Maeve. The only druid I've had the pleasure of meeting. And I will tell you the story of how Janice and I met Maeve," said Catherine proudly.

9 MAEVE

IT WAS THE BREAK OF DAWN. Janice the mouse and Catherine were packing all the supplies they would need for where they were heading to.

"Do we have bread?"

"Yes."

"Cheese?"

"Yes."

"Vegetables?"

"Yes."

"What else are we missing?"

"Don't worry I brought a knife just in case."

Both Janice and Catherine had started to walk down the hill from Catherine's hut. Most of the animals in the village were still asleep and they made sure no one noticed them leaving so early.

"You don't have to come with me, you know?"

"I know Janice, but I can't still let you go alone."

Both friends were walking northwest from the main entrance at Cecily Hill road. Catherine looked back and wondered what the others will say when they find out they're not in the village.

They walked numerous hours until they reached Sapperton, another village, in the outskirts west of Cirencester. They decided that it would be a good idea to take a small break before moving forward. Catherine opened her bag, laid a small picnic blanket, and took out the food.

"Do you reckon its true what they say?" asked Catherine.

"About what?" asked Janice with her mouth full of cheese and bread.

"Well about the spirits, and ghouls that live beyond Sapperton and Edgeworth."

Janice continues eating and ponders on what Catherine said.

"If a ghoul, spirit, witch or warlock comes between me and that magic water, they'd be sorry they crossed me."

Janice pulls out the knife from Catherine's bag and starts waving it around. Catherine slightly giggles.

"Going to stab a ghost, are you?" asked Catherine.

"Catherine, this is the last chance we got, we tried everything, every herb and root we could find, and my father is not getting better."

"We're bound to find something, so don't you fret! We've heard from the birds and other passing animals that there's something in the deep in the forest that can heal anyone, we just have to find it," said Catherine.

Janice hears what Catherine says, she straightens her back, nods in agreement and quickly re-packs.

"How long do you think it will take Socrates to find out that we left?" asked Catherine.

"Who knows, but I paid no attention to his warnings of the forest, I have my priorities," replied Janice.

It was nearly sunset, and Catherine and Janice were somewhere between the villages of Througham and Syde, northwest of Cirencester.

"Janice, do you know where we are?" asked Catherine.

"Perhaps," replied Janice

"What do we do now? We're lost and it's going to get dark soon."

Catherine was starting to worry that they've been walking for hours and they still haven't found anything that could resemble the healing water that they heard so much about.

Nightfall was slowly approaching; the forest was so thick and the dark clouds made it difficult to see.

They continued to walk in the forest and at times they felt they weren't alone as if something or someone was observing them. The wind was blowing forcefully and carried sounds that frightened them both.

"We must pick up the pace, I do not want to face danger," added Janice.

They were both very tired, but it was Janice's eagerness that motivated them. Then, out of nowhere, they both heard something peculiar, something they wouldn't expect to hear that deep in the woods. They heard a soft chime of bells. All of sudden, lightning strikes the sky, and it starts to rain densely. However, they could still hear the bell chimes.

"We need to find cover!" says Catherine loudly. The rain made it difficult for them to communicate.

"I'm not sure if I'm going mad, but can you hear a soft bell chime?!" asked Janice.

"Oh, thank goodness! I thought I was going mad myself! Yes! Yes, I can hear them as well!"

"Let's follow that sound!"

Visibility was difficult, but thankfully they were able to identify a hollow tree trunk. They both ran over muddy water towards the tree trunk to cover themselves from the rain. They entered the tree swiftly from the opening at the base. Once inside they were breathing fast-paced; they tried to gather their breath and took a moment to gather their thoughts.

"Right." Catherine is looking at the rain and catching her breath at the same time. "I say we stay here for the night, and start fresh tomorrow."

"I'm not sure whether to continue or head back," said Janice in a disappointing tone.

"We'll do what you decide is best, ok? Don't worry about me, we just have to get some sleep," said Catherine.

That night both Janice and Catherine stayed inside the hollow tree and in a matter of minutes they quickly went sound to sleep sitting next to each other.

The next morning, they both woke up to the warmth of the sun shining over their faces. Once fully up, Catherine opened the bag of snacks and gave Janice some biscuits for her to eat. Breakfast was small but sufficient. Finishing what they had to eat, they both stepped outside the tree and saw that they were surrounded by butterflies and beautiful patches of different coloured flowers. The branches of the trees sliced the sun beams that glimmered over the clear and soft mist that hovered gently over the ground, and they felt an overwhelming sense of calm."

"This part of the forest isn't too bad, Janice," said Catherine.

"It's actually not, Catherine, but I think we should go back. I'm sorry I brought you all the way out here. I thought it would be easier to find the medicine," said Janice while slowly getting her items with a disappointed face.

"Are you girls looking for medicine?"

Both Janice and Catherine were gobsmacked to hear a third voice. "Who could it be", they thought. They turned around to see who it was and standing next to the tree was a female human wearing a simple light brown tunic. She was wearing different pieces of jewellery most uncommon but interesting, to say the least. But the most absorbing piece of jewellery was her necklace. She was wearing the symbol of the Triskele, the symbol of druid. Her hair was fiery red and her eyes were bright green, almost mesmerizing.

Janice was a little shaky wondering why the giant was such in a calm mood to hear them speak, but Catherine kept on looking at her necklace; she knew the meaning of that symbol.

"Who are you?! Why are you talking to us?! What medicine?! asked Janice paranoically.

"Seems like awful lot of questions, little mouse, wouldn't you say so? Besides what are you doing in my forest?" replied the witty human.

Janice was mumbling her words and couldn't say nothing coherent.

"Hello, gentle human, my name is Catherine and my excited friend here is Janice."

"Nice to meet you both, my name is Maeve, and this all here, well, it's my forest".

"This forest doesn't belong to you! It belongs to the animals!" replied Janice angrily.

"Does it, now?" replied Maeve in a very amusing way. "Judging by your accent, both of you come from Cirencester. You are a bit far from home, girls."

"Yes, we live in Cirencester and, yes, we are a bit far from home!" replied Janice defensively.

"I see, so, what brings you here?" asked Maeve.

Janice and Catherine are silent.

"So, any answers?" asked Maeve.

"We are here because we are looking for a magic water that supposedly cures anyone. We were told by passing animals that it would be around these parts, somewhere in this forest," said Janice.

Maeve is silent.

"What are you going to do to us?" asked Catherine.

"Hmm, me? Nothing of course; besides today is a beautiful morning, is it not? I am guessing both of you are hungry, I can tell by your wet clothes that both of you had a bit of a rough night. Why don't you follow me to my hut for breakfast?" Maeve starts to walk the other direction.

"We already had breakfast, thank you," said Janice in a very untrustworthy tone to Maeve as she walked.

"I may know a thing or two about what you are looking for," replied Maeve.

Catherine and Janice looked at each other thinking what they should do. Catherine had a good feeling about her and wanted to risk it. As her grandmother would say: "Always follow your gut." But Janice, on the other hand, was more sceptical. At the end, they decided to accept the invitation to her hut. As they walked beside her, they both carefully observed the way she dressed, the way she looked. She was young, exceptionally beautiful, she emitted a sense calm that Catherine picked up right away. Maeve wasn't wearing any shoes; she wore bracelets on her wrists and ankles, some of them seemed to be made of silver and of wood that she probably carved. Her clothes looked old but clean; you could tell she had a young spirit.

By the time they reached Maeve's home, they noticed that it was in a thicker part of the woods. Her hut seemed similar to those of the animals of the forest, large and round, the roof was made up of mud and straw to keep the warmth in, and the walls were made up of stone and clay. There were no windows and, instead of a door, there was a cloth hanging.

"Please come in," said Maeve.

Maeve walked in and welcomed Janice and Catherine inside. They noticed an old rustic cauldron over the fire pit in the middle of the room. The fire pit was lit and they saw the reflection of the flames on the bronze shields that were hanging on the walls. There was a bed, a long table with several heavy books on it, they were old and dusty. They contained information on spells and herbal medicine. And next to the books were scientific instruments that Maeve would use on a regular basis. Next to the tables there were wooden boxes filled with jars that had different types of herbs and liquids.

"Will you ladies be so kindly to take a seat there by the table? I'm going to fetch us some tea," said Maeve.

Catherine and Janice did as they were told and hopped onto two stools. Maeve walked towards the cauldron and stirred the tea with the ladle. She grabbed two bowls that were on the floor and poured the tea in, then walked back to the table where the milk was and sat down with Catherine and Janice.

"I'm afraid I do not have teacups for animals, but I think the bowls should suffice," said Maeve as she sipped on her tea.

"So, where were we? Ah, yes, the medicine water, what have you heard about it?" asked Maeve.

"Not very much, only that it can be found these parts," responded Catherine.

"My father, you see, he is sick, and we need the water, we have tried to use every healing herb there is," added Janice.

"I see... have you tried teas like stinging nettle?"
"Yes."
"Milkweed?"
"Yes."
"Tree bark?"
"Yes."
"Lily flowers?"
"Yes."
"I see."

Maeve sighs and takes another sip of her tea.

"So, Janice, tell me what exactly is wrong with your father?" asked Maeve.

"He has been having trouble breathing, we think he may be under a dark spell."

"How long has he been like this?"

"Well, for the last month or so; we have tried about everything at this point."

"I see."

Maeve continued drinking her tea and smiled at the girls.

"Who are you, Maeve?" asked Janice.

"I thought you would have figured it out by now, it seems that your friend Catherine already has figured it out," replied Maeve.

Janice turns a look at Catherine and sees that her eyes are locked on the Triskelion symbol.

"Catherine, what's wrong?" asked Janice, as she shook her shoulder to break the trance that had grasped her.

"She's a druid! Merlin's beard, she's a druid!" said Catherine in an anxious manner.

"How do you know that?" asked Janice.

Maeve chuckles. "She knows because she is reacting to my pendant, this is the sign of Merlin, and her reaction means that she is sensitive to magic."

"Sorry? But, how do you mean I am sensitive to magic?" asked Catherine.

"Wait, if you're a druid, then you may have an idea about how we can get our hands on the medicine," interrupted Janice.

"Possibly," replied Maeve.

"POSSIBLY?!" remarked Janice. "Well, look here, you human or druid! I am not afraid of you! One way or another I will get that medicine for my father; mark my words!" said Janice.

"Calm yourself, my dear mouse. I only ask two things in return."

"And what would those two things be?" asked Janice.

"One, not to mention to any other animal that I am here, except for Socrates, he knows about me."

"How do you know Socrates?" asked Catherine.

"I'm a druid, remember; also, I am very aware of Alistair and the trouble he has been causing.

"Deal, once we get the medicine water we will be on our way and never talk about this again," said Janice excitingly.

"Why don't you want the other animals of the forest to know about you?" asked Catherine.

"I am one of the last druids who follows the old teachings of Merlin. I need not to draw attention to myself. I better serve animals from a distance," said Maeve.

Janice stops drinking her tea and stares at Maeve.

"How is it that we're meeting a druid for the first time till now? Weren't the druids hunted down by other humans in the past?" asked Janice.

"Correct, most of us were hunted down, burned, hung, drowned, stoned, tortured, what have you, but the remaining of us are in hiding and we blend in with other humans; we live amongst them, and sometimes even work with them. I just prefer to be in the forest. You see, not all humans are evil creatures, they simply fear what they do not understand. My purpose is to serve those who belong to the forest and nature as well to humans, so there can be a coexistence."

"And what is the second condition?" asked Janice.

"I would like to pass down some of my knowledge to Catherine."

"And why do you want to share your knowledge with me?!" asked Catherine in a surprised way.

"There are some animals and humans that can be taught magic. I knew you could be taught the moment you were drawn to my pendant, the Triskelion. I have always wanted to teach an animal some of my knowledge. I will only show you the easy stuff, what do you say?" asked Maeve.

"I haven't the slightest clue, how long will this take?" asked Catherine.

"For what I want to show you, about two days," said Maeve.

"Do we have two days?" asked Catherine to Janice.

"As long as we get that medicine," said Janice.

"Lovely! Let's get to work then and the medicine is yours."

Later that evening, Janice and Catherine were sitting in the middle of Maeve's hut. She wasn't home, she had left to pick up berries for dinner.

"So … two days," said Janice to herself.

"It seems so, although I am not sure what to expect, I never saw myself learning any type of magic," replied Catherine.

"All I can say is thank you, thank you for doing this, this will save my father," said Janice.

Janice and Catherine hugged each other around the fire, both wanting to get back home. Seconds later Maeve popped into her hut.

"Hello, girls, I hope the both of you are comfortable. I brought berries. Catherine, tomorrow early in the morning I will teach you simple magic. So, I need you to rest."

The morning after, Maeve and Catherine were outside the hut learning different spells and herbal medicine. Janice was sound asleep for she had too many berries. In a truly short time, Catherine learned to make potions and teas that were vital for the health. She even learned a couple of incantations to light up dark places or to help someone rest and have a delightful sleep. Catherine was knackered after those 48 hours of intensive training but was grateful that she learned it.

On the third day Maeve came back to the hut with different types of berries. She filled a couple of bowls and laid them on the ground so Janice and Catherine could eat by the fire pit.

Maeve sits with them and stares into the fire and clears her throat.

"Janice dear?"

"Yes, Maeve?"

Maeve puts her hand into her satchel and takes out a very small flask a bright blue light. Both girls stop eating and stares at it with awe.

"This is called the Elixir of Revival, just add them into the tea your father is drinking and in a matter of minutes, his illness will pass."

Maeve gracefully hands Janice the flask and Janice thanks Maeve multiple times for what she is receiving. She is very grateful and apologizes for the manner she had behaved with her previously.

"I have sent a message to the owls to come pick you up both as soon as possible so you can heal your father."

"Thank you, Maeve, thank you," says Janice.

"It is my pleasure to help an animal that has shown such bravery. Also, you mustn't use all of the medicine because there is something else I will need to ask of you," said Maeve.

"Oh? Of me? What would that be?" asked Janice.

"One day you will not have the need to use this anymore. One day you shall pass this flask along to someone who you think will need it. Just follow your heart and, if it feels right, pass along the flask.

"You have yourself a deal, Maeve." Janice extended her hand and shook Maeve's finger to conclude the transaction.

The following morning the three of them were standing outside the hut. The sun was rising, and the scenery was beautiful. The trees were tall dark and green, and they admired the sight of flowers and butterflies.

"Janice, when you get back to your village, you cannot say that you met me, say that you came across the flask in a stream, I must remain isolated," said Maeve.

"I promise to keep your identity and location a secret," responded Janice.

"Thank you, child," replied Maeve.

Moments later the three of them could see Socrates landing in front of them.

"Janice and Catherine, I thought I told the both of you not to wander into the forest. These are not safe times," said Socrates.

"You need not to worry Socrates, they have my blessing and I have given them the medicine for Janice's father; they know my conditions," said Maeve.

"Thank you, Maeve, you are far too kind," replied Socrates.

Before taking off to Cirencester, the four of them discussed on how Socrates and Maeve knew each other and the importance of Maeve's whereabouts and location be undisclosed. If either of Catherine or Janice ever wondered if there was a more beyond Cirencester, well, now they knew.

10 THE TRUTH

AS CATHERINE FINISHED telling her story outside her home, no one said anything. Everyone was happy that Sarah was going to get well, but now their curiosity was focused on Catherine.

"Is everyone alright?" asked Catherine. Jasper was completely shocked knowing that her mother kept this secret from him for such a long time and everyone else was so silent that they could hear the wind rustle against the leaves.

Socrates clears his throat to draw attention to himself. "I believe we have all had a difficult night, it is safe to say that Sarah will be fine tomorrow in the morning, for the two of you. Collin, may you accompany Eileen to her home and see no harm comes her way?"

"Of course, Socrates, and to you, Catherine, may you rest. Jasper, I'll see you tomorrow," said Collin.

"Thank you for your help Catherine, I am forever grateful," said Eileen. Both had started to walk back home.

"I will take my leave as well, Catherine, I will come back tomorrow to see the progress of Sarah's health. Good night, dear," said Socrates.

"Good night, old friend," replied Catherine.

It was now only Jasper and Catherine outside.

"Why didn't you tell me that a druid trained you? What else haven't you told me?" Jasper had so many questions and didn't know where to start.

Catherine looked at Jasper and gave him a hug. Jasper had always got used to his mother being strong and assertive, so showing affection through a hug was new to him.

"I am sorry that I didn't tell you before; I believe it is time you knew the truth about your brother, but today is not the day for that conversation. Come, grab some carrots and biscuits and rest up. We'll speak tomorrow."

The next morning Eileen was walking from her hut towards Catherine's home. It was a sunny day, and the birds were chirping joyously. She did not converse with them because all that she had on her mind was her mother and if whether she would be awake today or not.

By the time she approached Catherine's house, she gently knocked on the door nervously. Catherine opened the door and greeted her good morning.

"Would you like to see her?" asked Catherine with a gentle smile.

"May I?" replied Eileen nervously.

Catherine allows Eileen to come in. The first thing she sees is her mother having morning breakfast tea with Jasper. Eileen heart is filled with delight and relief that she quickly goes over to her to hug her.

"I thought you were going to die." Eileen starts to tear up as she is holding her mother ever so tightly.

"Everything is fine, sweetie, the worst has passed, come sit down with us and have a cup of tea. Jasper made a delicious brew," said Sarah.

Catherine comes to the table with a teacup and saucer, and Jasper pours a cuppa for Eileen.

"Do you know what's my favourite part of having tea is, Eileen?" asked Catherine.

"No, what is it?" replied Eileen.

"That no matter the occasion, happy, sad, good news or bad, there will always be tea; thank the stars that today is a happy occasion," said Catherine.

"Indeed, it is," said Sarah.

"So, how is everyone's morning?" asked Eileen in a now better and optimistic tone of voice.

"Well, dear, before you came, Jasper here was telling me all different kinds of mischievous stories of his adventures with Collin; who knew Jasper had a daring spirit," said Sarah.

"It's hard to keep an eye on this one," said Catherine chuckling.

"Mother, how are you feeling? Are you alright to come back home?" asked Eileen.

"Why yes, let's just finish our tea so we can head back on home. Catherine and Jasper have been more than helpful.

The rest of the morning the four of them continued drinking their tea with much delight. They talked about the events that occurred the night before, about how all the animals of the forest decided to stop fighting each other and work together. Soon after breakfast Sarah and Eileen thanked Catherine and Jasper for all their help and hospitality. They departed home. As soon as they left, Catherine looked at Jasper.

"Now we can have that conversation," said Catherine.

"I could not mention Maeve to you because I made a promise to her that I wouldn't reveal her identity to anyone else. And last night I broke that promise for the second time."

"When was the first time?"

"With your brother."

Jasper scratches his chin.

"What does my brother have to do with the druid you met?"

"When your brother was younger, and before you were born, he was the first one I told him about what magic was. As he grew older, he became obsessed with it. Our arguments were about me wanting to teach him magic and me telling him how to find Maeve. Multiple times he went out to look for Maeve in the forest and every time he went, he never found her."

"Then what happened?"

"One day your brother said he needed to go to London. I asked him why on earth he needed to go there? He said he finally knew where to find what he was looking for. And in the wee hours of the morning, he was gone. By the time I alerted Socrates that your brother was missing, it was too late. The owls searched far and wide for him; they never found him."

"Did my brother mention anything else?" asked Jasper intriguingly.

"He mentioned a place called the 'Phoenix'. That was where he was off to. I didn't understand what he meant to say by it."

Jasper did not know what to say; his heart was rushing. He was not scared, anxious or upset, but overwhelmed with all this new information.

"I need to go to London. I need to find my brother."

Catherine simply stares at Jasper. "Do you realize what I am trying to tell you? Your brother went off to some obscure idea in his mind and hasn't returned in years! I will not lose you too!"

"I need to save my brother, London will burn ... I have seen it in my dreams. You have always told me that our dreams have meanings, and we should not ignore them. William is alive and in London," said Jasper.

Catherine has a knot in her throat and cannot find the right words to express herself. She wants to see her other son, but she does not want to see Jasper go off and never return.

"Mum?"

"You will stay in Cirencester. I cannot let you make the same mistake your brother did and that is final."

"Why haven't the owls gone to London if they know where he is then!" Jasper starts to raise his voice.

"Because Alistair is there!" said Catherine in a louder voice.

Neither of them said a word for a moment. Jasper finds courage to confront the topic of Alistair. "I am tired of no one telling us who Alistair is! What does a falcon have to do with my brother?" asked Jasper.

Catherine takes a big sigh. "The night your brother left, Socrates came to me, ashamed. He felt he was partly responsible of the departure of your brother. I don't know why, but Socrates told me your brother went to confront Alistair. Socrates did not tell me why he wanted to do so. Regardless of why he went, I was ready to go to London myself to get my son back; I was ready to fight against all odds just to get William home. But Socrates and the owls stopped me before I could leave my home. They told me I would perish the moment Alistair had a hold of me. There is a pact that maintains the peace in the forest, Socrates does not go London, and Alistair does not come to the forest. London is his city, and there are more animals like him."

Catherine got up from the table and walked outside the kitchen. The rest of the day Jasper and Catherine did not speak to each other. When Jasper finally went to sleep the only thing that was going in his mind was how was he going to get to London.

The next morning Jasper went walking towards Collin's hut. He arrived at his posh home and knocked on the door. Collin opened the door still in his pyjamas yawning and stretching his arms.

"Good morning, old friend, how does fate treat you today?"

"I'm off to London, Collin. I am going to go find my brother and bring him back."

"You are going to do what now exactly?" asked Collin trying to comprehend what he just heard.

"My mum and I finally spoke about the past, the real past. With all the dreams that I have been having, I believe it is time I did something about it."

"Are you proper mad today? Did you hit your head with something? When and how will are you planning on going to London? You do realize the humans are having a bloody war and you want to go were all the action is?"

"Tomorrow early in the morning I'm leaving. I came to say goodbye and thank you. I haven't planned it out yet, but things tend to work themselves out, yeah?"

"You do realize how far London is? You can't be serious mate."

"Goodbye, Collin."

Jasper paid no attention to what Collin was telling him. Collin just saw Jasper walking down from his hill.

That same morning Jasper kept on walking in the middle of the forest thinking about how would he get to London, where would he stop on the way, what should he bring, how many days or weeks would this take? One thing he knew for sure was that Socrates could not know, or he would stop him from leaving.

He finally reached Eileen's home. He gently knocked on the door. Eileen opened the door and her face brightened as the sun shined on her.

"Jasper? Hello, how are you? Would you like to come in?"

Jasper focused on her beautiful emerald green eyes. He saw kindness in those eyes, but he was sad because he wouldn't know when he would look at her again.

"I would love to, Eileen, but right now is not the moment."

"Is everything all right?"

"Yes, everything is fine, I just came to tell you that I will be leaving the forest for some time. I am unaware of my return, or if I will ever return for that matter. I felt that I had to let you know."

"Where are you off to?"

"I rather not say. But it has something to do with my brother."

"Oh ... ok."

"Yes."

Eileen hugs Jasper tightly, she places her paw on his face.

"Don't do get yourself killed, Jasper Jones."

Jasper turns around without saying anything and walks towards home. As he is walking down a tear runs down his face. His emotions are divided. He does not want to leave his friends and mother, but if he does not try and save his brother, then that will be a feeling of regret he will carry for the rest of his life.

11 LEAVING THE VILLAGE

SEPTEMBER 4TH LANDED on a Wednesday. It was 5 in the morning, and Jasper was wide awake. He was in his room with his old rucksack; inside there was food, old maps of the countryside, a knife and water. He was being overly cautious in not to make any noise so he would not disturb his mother. He knew if he told her where he was off to, she would forbid it.

He stepped out of the room and walked directly towards the door. Before opening the door, he took a long and deep breath. He knew the moment he would step outside he would go straight towards London. He nervously opened the door slowly and stepped out. To his surprise was his mother sitting on the same stone she sat on when she told the story of Maeve.

"Are you off already?"

"I thought you were asleep. I didn't wake you up because I didn't want to disturb you."

"I'm not going to stop you from going to London, but I will ask you one thing."

"What is it?"

Catherine stood up and walked towards Jasper to give him the strongest hug she had ever given him in his whole life.

"Whatever happens, be safe and come back."

Jasper held his mother tightly.

"Before you head off, I want to give you something that might help you on your journey."

Catherine fished out a light blue stone that fitted perfectly within her palm and was not heavy. She gave have it to Jasper.

"The distance from here to London is quite far, you are going to meet other animals on the way, some may be good, some may be bad. Not all animals speak truth, and you will find them in a bigger city. If an animal lies to you or has some intention of harming you, that stone will shine blue as a warning. This stone was given to me by Maeve."

He thanked his mother, he fixed his flat cap pulled up his back sack and walked towards south of Cirencester. Why did Jasper walk south if London was west of the countryside? Because he was going to take a short cut which no other animal of the forest has taken in the past.

Jasper was heading towards Kemble, a smaller village than Cirencester. The distance is long for an animal. Jasper did not know how to access the secret tunnels by himself, reaching Kemble from Cirencester was going to take 3 or 4 hours walking. And indeed, he walked.

By the time Jasper was halfway towards Kemble, all he could think about was how he would get to London, or if whether there would be other stopping points on the way. He was incredibly careful on rationing food and drink; he was also thinking if he would be able to find food along the way. There were many uncertainties, but he pressed on.

He had already crossed one of the main roads, Tetbury Road and was now approaching part of the River Thames. He was told by one of the birds that when he reached part of the river Thames, Kemble would not be so far. He took out his water canteen out refill it.

Jasper decided that this would be a good time to catch his breath and reanalyse his plan. To be completely honest, there wasn't much of a plan at all; never had he been this far from his village and there were no specific steps on how to get to London from Kemble.

Jasper's plan arriving to Kemble is to take the train. The problem is that he has never been on one or seen one. When he asked the birds what was the fastest way to get to London they would talk about the train and they would describe it as a mechanical beast that roared whenever it moved. It would pump out black smoke from the front as it went forward. There would be a couple of stops here and there, but it will arrive to London.

Before continuing on his journey, he heard distant voices behind him. He turned back and looked. There were some trees, bushes and a hill, but he saw no one. He reached down his bag to retrieve his knife. He knew the further away he walked from Cirencester, the more likely he might confront other animals that might want to hurt him or eat him.

"Who goes there? Show your faces! I am not afraid!"

There was no response. Jasper continued to look where those sounds were coming from. Right before he disregarded the situation and continued to walk towards Kemble, there was something coming from over the hill that caught his attention.

Surprisingly, it was Collin and Eileen running as fast as they could towards Jasper. "Had they come to stop him?" he thought.

"Where do you think you're going without us, old bean?" asked Collin.

"You're going to London and not going to invite us? Seems a bit rude if you ask me," said Eileen.

"So, neither of you have come to take me back to the village?" asked Jasper.

"Take you back? We have been trying to catch up with you since you left the village in the morning. We want to come with you," said Collin.

"I couldn't ask neither of you to come with me, it's too dangerous. I think I know where my brother is and I'm off to bring him back. And to make matters worse it appears the evil falcon, Alistair, is also involved here," said Jasper.

"Well then, that's fine, he doesn't know us does he? All we need to do is get your brother and go by undetected," said Collin.

"It's not that simple," replied Jasper.

"Sure it is, stop trying to convince us that go back. We're here, the three of us go to London and coming back with a fourth, your brother," added Eileen.

"Thank you, to the both of you," said Jasper.

"Well, let's not get emotional here. I would rather prefer if we could get to Kemble as soon as possible. I do not want to be another animals' dinner. By the way Jasper, I am intrigued to know what is your plan?" asked Collin.

Jasper was silent.

"We do have a plan right?" asked Collin for a second time.

12 KEMBLE

JASPER, COLLIN, AND EILEEN arrived to Kemble by the time the sun was setting. They could see there were more uniformed humans running all over the place as if they were preparing for the war. There were crates of weapons and ammunition being hauled from one place to the other. Orders were being given from left and right as the soldiers carried them out.

"Do you think this has something to do with what we all saw in the fire the day after the summer solstice?" asked Eileen.

"I'm not sure, but we need to find that mechanical beast and hop on it so we can get to London as quick as possible," said Jasper.

"Does this train … speak? How does it actually works?" asked Collin.

"I'm sure we will find out soon enough," responded Jasper.

The three of them made sure they would wander around Kemble unnoticed by the humans, but they already seem too busy. In matter of fact, they were down Windmill Road, and the surrounding trees and bushes were perfect for cover. They passed several lovely houses and cottages that gave a sense of warmness and cosiness. Down the road they came upon an intersection, decided to take a right turn as it seemed the road was leading further into the middle of the town.

"Jasper, I reckon we need to stay the night in one of these houses, it's going to be dark very soon and we must not expose ourselves," said Collin.

Jasper did not want to take a break, he wanted to keep on going, but at the same time he knew that Collin was right, taking unnecessary risks could jeopardize the whole mission.

"Let's go to a pub for a couple of pints so we can plan the next steps," said Eileen. They were now on Station Road, walking and looking for a place where they could spend the night. They came across a small pub called the Lions Den. They were a little hesitant to enter because it was filled with humans and were not sure if there would be a secret passage way for animals.

"Pst...Psst...PSSST!"

They all looked back to see it was a shrew that was calling them. He looked like a peculiar character, he was calling them from a garden and waiving them to come in.

"Are you three, bloody crazy?! What are you doing out on the streets!"

"Hello and good evening, pardon our rudeness but who are you, friend?" asked Collin.

"My name is Drew! You three should not be outside or they will come?!"

"Who, the humans? They're too busy with their own business they won't notice us," said Collin.

"No! Not the humans! Forget about the humans!"

"Then what is the problem? Who should we be afraid of?" asked Eileen.

"The FOXES! The bloody foxes! You need to hide yourselves quickly!"

They remembered that foxes can easily adapt to any environment and they can be quite active around dusk.

"Where can we hide Drew the Shrew?" Jasper and Eileen giggled as Collin said his full name. Drew just rolled his eyes upwards.

"Anywhere! Beware of the Pack! The name of the leader is Jack." Jasper was curious to hear that the name Jack rhymed with the word "pack". He never heard such a thing before.

"Well, well, what do we have here, eh?" asked a voice coming from behind. Two foxes appeared from the dark and slowly approached the rabbits and the shrew.

"Drew, is this how you greet outsiders to our lovely village? Not very kind of you speaking about the foxes that way," said the second fox with a sly tone.

Jasper could not remember when was the last time he saw an actual fox. They both wore rugged grey flat caps and old scarfs around their necks, though their vests were very dashing and stylish. Drew was so scared that he just froze.

"Of course, not Billy, err I — "

"No, no, don't Billy me, Drew, I wonder how will Jack react when he finds out that someone in his village is mal-talking about the Pack. Now, you don't want to hurt Jacks feelings, right? We all know what happens when Jacks feelings gets hurt," said the first fox.

Drew just nodded in agreement.

"Well then ... Drew ... I suggest you crawl back into the hole where you came from!" said the second fox with a snarl.

Drew did not say a single word and dug the fastest hole a shrew could ever dig.

"Ahem, allow us to introduce ourselves," said the second fox. "My name is Billy, Billy the fox and this my associate, Reginald, we call him Reggie for short."

The three rabbits stood there trying to think of a plan on how to escape.

"Now, now, don't be thinking of running off, we would loathe and detest running after you ... that's if you can run fast enough."

The three rabbits were all thinking the same thing, and they did exactly what the foxes told them not to do. So, they ran.

"After them!" said Reggie.

The rabbits were sprinting down Station Road as fast as they could. They ran towards a more populated area of human soldiers carrying weapons and crates. From where they were they could see smoke appearing and hear a large hiss.

"That's gotta be the train! Let's see if we can hop on it!" said Collin.

They now had a clear view of the station and could clearly see the train and size of it. As they ran, Eileen looked back and saw that Reggie and Billy were coming in hot right behind them. All the humans were so busy with their duties that they paid no attention to the chase. The rabbits were running alongside the tracks, but right before they could reach the platform a third fox jumped right in front of them preventing them to move on any further.

"Well, good evening," said the third fox

"Bollocks!" cried Collin.

"How rude," replied the third fox.

"Gave these rabbits here a fair warning of not running off, boss," said Billy.

"I don't Adam & Eve it," said the third fox.

The three rabbits looked at each other in confusion.

"Are you Jack? The leader of the Pack?" asked Jasper.

"Correct and you three are in barney rubble," said Jack.

None of the rabbits could understand a word Jack was saying.

"Let's take a ball & chalk, rabbits," said Jack.

"That means let's take a walk. A walk back to our place," said Reggie.

The rabbits and the three foxes were now walking south of Kemble to the open fields. They were being led towards their fox holes and, on their way, Reggie and Billy were explaining to the rabbits that Jack was a fox born in East London, and humans and animals speak in rhyme from that part of the city, also known as cockney rhyme and slang. But this explanation did not make Jack's way of talk more understandable to the rabbits.

"Why are you taking us back to your burrows?" asked Eileen.

"We're going to see what plans Jack has for the you lot."

13 JACK AND HIS PACK

DEEP IN THE FOX HOLE where the Pack resided, the three rabbits found themselves sitting in a on a cold floor with Reggie, who watched over them very closely. There wasn't much in the fox hole to be honest: it was damp, cold and wet, nothing compared with the tunnels in Cirencester. However, it was a pretty big fox hole.

Jack went on looking for his brother Kevin.

"Kevin! Kevin … Kev—. Oh, bloody hell, where is my brother? Reggie have you seen him?"

"Haven't, boss, he must be somewhere."

Jasper and Collin were looking at each other already trying come up with a plan. They were not too far from the train station in Kemble but, if they tried to escape the foxes would surely catch up. They needed a distraction of some sort.

"Well, let's get down to business; judging by the looks of you and the way you talk, I reckon you're from Cirencester," affirmed Jack.

"That is correct," replied Jasper.

"Well, what would three little rabbits be doing so far from home? Rumour has it that things are not going so well in the village?" asks Jack in a very sly manner.

"The village has seen better days; panic has fallen over out forest. My good fox, we are simple travellers on a mission; how about you let us loose." replies Collin.

"Don't try to act smart with me, the three of you are going to be here for a while." Reggie and Billy are snickering as Jack gets mad.

"Host, are you from Kemble?" asks Collin as he tries to sweet talk Jack.

"None of your business! The Pack and I be from East London. I am a Cockney fox! Rhyme and slang the way I talk! That's how we all talk, including the humans. But that shouldn't be a concern of yours, rabbit!"

Jasper's eye widened when he heard Jack mention London.

"You're from London? Please, Jack! My friends and I are meant to be in London! We need to get there before it's too late!" said Jasper.

"Well, it appears neither of you three will be going to London any time soon. Besides, what business would three country rabbits have there?" asked Jack.

"I need to get to the Phoenix, to save my brother before the whole city burns," said Jasper. Jack pauses for a moment and looks very closely at Jasper.

"Phoenix?! How do you know about the Phoenix?! Speak, rabbit, or I will not be merciful when I eat you," commands Jack in a menacing way.

Jasper realizes that maybe he shouldn't have mentioned the Phoenix.

"All I know is that my brother is there, and some falcon called Alistair is there as well. But I couldn't care less about the falcon. I just want to save my brother, and be back at the village," said Jasper.

"I see." Jack squints his eyes. "Perhaps I shall tell you a little bit more of the Phoenix. It is a club where all the street animals congregate, it is a den for thieves, muggers and pick pocketers. It is not for the fainted of heart, especially not for three rabbits from the west country. The Phoenix used to belong to me! Property of the Pack! That was of course before Alistair came and banished us from London. That rotten falcon took away what belongs to me!" yelled Jack.

"Great! So, if you let us go, we will be on our way, and maybe we can get your club back," said Collin in a nervous manner.

"That be most unwise, rabbit," said Jack as Reggie and Billy started to slowly approach the rabbits. Their teeth and nails were showing and ready.

"You see, there are two scenarios if your brother is in the Phoenix; one: either your brother works for Alistair, and he is part of the theft of the Phoenix, and that we cannot allow that to go unforgiven and you must pay for his actions, or two: he is a prisoner of Alistair, which most of them end up dead. And if you go, it's most likely Alistair will have you meet the same fate," said Jack.

"I'll take my chances," said Jasper.

"Well, I don't think we will, let's eat up, boys!" said Jack!" Right before Jack launched over the rabbits, Reginald had a question.

"Jack! Hold on a minute, the grey rabbit said something about London on fire? I'm a bit curious, can you ask him about that?" asked Reginald.

Jack takes a big sigh.

"Alright, alright, well, rabbit, what's this about London being on fire, and hurry it up, keep it short so we can eat you lot," said Jack.

"I do not know exactly."

"Eat em!" interrupted Jack.

"Wait, wait, but I have seen it in my dreams. That is why I need to save my brother before it's too late," says Jasper in a serious tone.

The foxes all start to laugh at Jasper.

"Ooooh, I can see visions in my dreams," said Reggie.

"Ooooh, I have been blessed by Merlin," said Billy.

"And what have you seen in your dreams...rabbit?" asked Jack

"The city will be engulfed by flames raining down the sky," said Jasper

The foxes continue to laugh it out even harder.

"Oh, I do love a good laugh before we dinner, but never have I had my dinner made me laugh before having it. Do you realize how big the city of London is? And to set it all up on fire ... " Jack continues to laugh.

"Look, if you let us go, we promise we will never come back to Kemble, but I need to get on that train!" said Jasper.

"How can a city like London just disappear?" Chuckles Jack.

The Pack had cornered the three rabbits, there was no plan and no escape. Then the most unexpected thing happened.

"Helloooo? Laaaaads? Aaaaare you inside?"

"Ugh! Its Kevin, could he have not come in later?" said Billy.

"Why can't we just eat them and get over with it?" asked Reggie.

"Quiet! The both of you!" snarled Jack. "We're in here, Kevin! Come on down!"

Coming into the fox hole arrives Kevin, Jack's younger brother. He was rather a robust fox with round cheeks and bright red fur. His face and his fat belly were covered in strawberry jam and butter as he was chewing on a pastry.

"What do we have here, lads?"

"Innit obvious? Its dinner," said Billy.

Jack sighs. "Where were you?! And what are you eating, Kevin? Look at your fur! You're covered in ... in ... jam! What am I going to do with you?", says Jack as he puts his paw on his forehead.

"I got me one of the bakers jam tarts! You know what they say about jam tarts: jam tarts always make you fart!" said Kevin as he laughed out loud.

Reggie and Billy laugh at Kevin behind his back. Jack takes Kevin to speak with him in private.

"Ok, Kevin, do you remember what have we discussed before?" says Jack in serious tone.

"About being foxes?" asks Kevin,

"Yes."

"About hunting?"

"Yes."

"About eating ... other animals?"

"Yeees!"

"I'm not sure if I can eat another animal; pastries are so much better, plus they don't run away if you want to get one," says Kevin.

"Kevin! We are foxes! We hunt smaller pray! Ok?! So act like one!" Jack was getting annoyed with his brother. For a while, Jack has been trying to work with his younger brother on how to act like a real fox.

"Back to the matter at hand," says Kevin as he returns where he left off.

"Boss, should we get some cheese, bread or even vegetables?" asked Reggie.

"Yeah, boss, I don't think three tiny rabbits are going to fill us up; you know, we should garnishing them up to have a proper feast."

Jack was starting to lose his patience because all he wanted was to eat one of the rabbits.

"Fine! Fine! Ok, we will go into Kemble and come back with scraps, but I do not want any more delays! We come back, no more questions, we eat em' plain and simple."

Reggie and Billy agreed. Next to Jack there was a small rusty cage and right in there Jasper, Collin and Eileen were placed. Jack took his key from his coat and locked the door so they wouldn't escape.

"Kevin … I am going to place my trust in you, I need you to watch the rabbits, and make sure they do not leave. Can I trust you?" asked Jack.

"Oh, of course you can! How hard is it to watch three of rabbits?" said Kevin in a confident tone.

"I mean it, Kevin, we will go into town and come back. I'm taking the key. DO NOT LET THEM OUT OF YOUR SIGHT. IS THAT UNDERSTOOD?" asked Jack.

"Why of course, brother! Do not fret, and if you're going into town, can you bring me a cheese toasty?" asked Kevin very politely.

"NO CHEESE TOASTY! JUST WATCH THEM RABBITS!" snarled Jack to his brother Kevin. Jack, Reggie and Billy had left their underground hole towards Kemble and now Kevin was entrusted with the task to make sure the rabbits wouldn't escape. Now, Kevin tried very hard to pull different facial expressions as he stared into the rabbits eyes: he had a serious face, and a mean face, a face no to be reckon with, but he could not stay in character.

"Oh, boy, I do hope my brother comes back with a scrumptious toasty indeed!" said Kevin.

"Kevin, dear boy, you don't seem to be very much like your brother," said Collin as he sat in the cage.

"Me and my brother are very much alike, thank you very much! And my job is to watch over you three! So, no trickery!" replied Kevin.

"No trickery here, but you are far kinder than your brother, not as aggressive as he is. Do you hunt with the Pack?"

"Why of course I hunt, although sometimes we hunt for different things. I hunt for sticky toffee pudding, banoffee pie, artic rolls, jam roly-poly, Christmas pudding, bread and butter pudding, figgy pudding, custard tart, crumble, trifle, carrot cake, apple pie, summer pie, rhubarb pie, apple cake, especially apple cake, I adore a good apple cake."

"Do you hunt animals?" asked Eileen.

"I do not partake in such savagery," replied Kevin.

"Kevin, you seem like a kind fox; would you be so inclined to let us go?" asked Jasper.

"Oh, no, no, my brother Jack would not like that one single bit. He told me to watch you and that is what I would do! Hmph!" said Kevin as he stomped his foot.

"Do you fear your brother?" asked Collin.

"No, but I respect him. Ever since we were little foxes in London, he would do the impossible to protect me. We've been on our own for quite a while. He's all I have. And Reggie and Billy, we are all one big family."

"I know what you mean, Kevin," said Jasper.

"You do?!" Jasper has Kevin's attention.

"Do you know why we are in Kemble?"

"No."

"Us three are bound to London; we are off to save my brother. If he stays much longer in that city he is going to be in grave danger, I must bring him back to the village, and we need to get on the train from Kemble."

"Goodness gracious, I had no idea." Shocked was Kevin upon what he heard.

"Let us go, Kevin; I too respect my brother. What would you do if you were in my shoes?" asked Jasper.

"Well, if Jack was in trouble, I too would do the impossible to save him," responded Kevin.

There is a moment of silence between Kevin and Jasper. Kevin is thinking profoundly on what he should do.

"I have a knife, I can open the lock, you can say that we tricked you and overpowered you. If you let us go, we promise never to return to Kemble," said Jasper.

Kevin continues to hesitate, but eventually the kindness of his heart outweighs what his brother ordered him to do.

Kevin takes the stone out of his pocket, he wanted to know whether the stone would change colour to see if Kevin was lying. It turns out he was telling the truth, he was going to help them.

Jasper takes out his knife and places it in the lock. He slides it in and turns it around in different ways to see which would open the lock. After several minutes the lock is broken.

"Hurry before Jack comes back!" said Eileen.

From the entrance of the fox hole they could hear Jack and the lads coming back from their scavenger. They were singing a song on how they were going to eat Jasper and his friends.

"Oh, no! He's here!" said Collin.

The door of the cage opens.

"Where are we to go?!" asked Jasper.

"Follow me, there is another way out of here," said Kevin.

Kevin leads the rabbits to the other side of the fox hole that turned out to be an underground tunnel. By the time they reached the exit, Kevin didn't go any further.

"I leave you here, rabbits, by the time Jack is here I will make it seem that I am chasing you," said Kevin

"Thank you, Kevin, I will not forget your act of kindness," said Jasper.

"A real gentleman you are, may our paths cross again in the future!" said Collin.

"Thank you, Kevin, you are the best fox," said Eileen as she kissed him on the cheek. Kevin blushed for he had never been kissed. The three rabbits take off and start to pick up the pace.

"Run as fast as you can and don't turn back!" yelled Kevin.

The rabbits were now sprinting back towards Kemble, they were not so far now. From the distance, they could see smoke coming out of the train, humans were moving boxes in it, and it seemed it was about to move any minute now.

Over the hill that they just passed the rabbits could hear Jack's howl in anger. So, they moved with even more haste. The rabbits knew that foxes are quick animals and would be able to catch up easily.

"They're after us!" cried Eileen as she looked back. She saw Jack's eyes bloodshot red in anger. He and his Pack were starting to catch up. Kevin was having a hard time running behind Jack, Reggie and Billy, he couldn't run at the same speed.

"Almost there, pick up the pace!" cried Jasper!

The rabbits were now entering Kemble and outside of the train station, they could hear the train blowing its horn. They made their way onto the platform to board the train and avoid being spotted by the humans. Hiding behind a stack of packed barrels, they could see that one of the wagons slide door was still open.

"We must get in there!" said Collin.

"Don't let them get away!" yelled Jack.

But, before the foxes could continue with the chase, one of the young cadets that was loading boxes into the train noticed four foxes running. As he spotted them, he thought they would do nicely as target practiced. He alerted his companions to take out their pistols and see who could hit one or all of them.

Jasper, Eileen, and Collin sprinted from the platform into the wagon without being noticed by anyone. They were completely out of breath after the chase. Outside they could hear the sound of guns going off. Jasper and Collin peaked outside to see what was happening. The foxes were cornered, and so was Kevin. He was finally able to catch up with his brother. Their backs where up against crates, they had nowhere to go. They were blinded by the lights that shined on them. Five human soldiers were in position to execute the four foxes.

"We have to do something," yelled Eileen.

"We can't leave Kevin, he helped us," added Collin.

The train whistle blew and Jasper could hear the slide doors of other wagons closing. Jasper was already on the train, about to head to London. But now the fox that helped him needed help. He saw that, in the wagon they were in, there was several crates of barrels stacked together and being held by rope.

"I have an idea, quickly, we need to cut the rope!" said Jasper. Each rabbit went to one crate to cut and bite the rope. Jasper was using the knife that he had brought from home.

"Ready!" Jasper could hear a human soldier commencing the execution. They had started to cut the rope even faster.

"Aim!" They were almost there, they just needed to cut this last single thread. And right before the soldier could say 'fire' the barrels had started to roll out one by one out. Some of them broke as they were coming out, some just rolled off and continued to do so. This caught the attention of the majority of the soldiers that were working there.

The execution was halted right before the cadets could pull the trigger, and they went to help with the mess that was happening on the platform. By a second, the foxes could not believe how close they were. Jack saw all the soldiers trying to catch the barrels that were rolling; it was a mess. From a corner of the wagon Collin and Jasper peaked out and waved their hats to the foxes.

"Are we still alive?" asked Kevin.

"Yes, we are ... yes we are," responded Jack as he saw the rabbits waving and smiling.

One of the human captains gave the order to shut the slide door because they were behind schedule. And the slide door was shut and slowly the train had started to move.

Now the three rabbits could take a proper break from all the running they did.

"Let's hope the ride to London isn't as tiresome," said Jasper.

14 REMY AND TEMPLETON 'CRACKERS'

THE RABBITS PLACED their rucksacks in front of them and fell against the hay.

After a long day and almost being devoured by foxes, and then saving them, Jasper, Eileen and Collin would shut their eyes momentarily. They were tired and needed to gather up strength. As Jasper was slowly starting to close his eyes, he saw two blurry figures in front of him. He couldn't tell if he was starting to dream or if there were other animals in the wagon that they didn't know about.

This worried him. He was having trouble in getting up and with the little energy he had, he sat up and rubbed his eyes.

"Hurry, hurry, before they get up!" said one blurry figure.

"Let's see what goodies them rabbit have in here," whispered the other blurry figure. One was shorter than the other.

Gaining clear visibility, Jasper sees two rats meddling with his, Collin's and Eileen's rucksacks. Both of them were wearing punctured vests, baggy trousers and bowler hats.

"Stay away from our belongings! Collin, Eileen! Wake up!" Eileen awakens in a heartbeat, but Collin gets up less gracefully yawning and mumbling incoherent sentences, trying to figure out what is happening.

"Remy, they're awake!"

"We have to scram!"

Before the two rats can disperse, the three rabbits tackle them and pin both of them onto the ground.

"Oi! Get off me!" said the short rat.

"Yeah, why don't you pick on someone on your own size!" said the other rat.

"You were trying to steal our belongings!" said Eileen.

"Well, dear, may I ask, why have you and your friends intruded into our home!" replied the short rat.

"We did not know this was your home! Besides, it is a wagon!" said Eileen.

"Well … it's our wagon, we were here first and now you know! And get off of us!" said the other rat.

The rabbits and the rats look at each other waiting for someone to say or do something.

"Well? What are we supposed to do in this predicament, eh?" said the short rat in a sarcastic tone.

"Get off em," said Jasper.

As the rabbits got up, so did the rats. They were fixing their vest and bowler hats. They all took a good look at each other. The rats patted themselves down. The short rat clears his throat.

"Finally! How rude of you three to smuggle into our train, unannounced, and attack us! In our very home!" said the short rat.

"Well, you two should have known better not to meddle in other animals' belongings! And we did not know we were in your home! We were busy being chased by foxes and we needed to escape," said Eileen.

"Foxes, you say, you wouldn't mean you were chased by that Cockney bloke Jack, were you? Jack and his Pack?"

"Yes! That's him, the one who spoke in rhyme.

He would have made us their dinner if we wouldn't have made into this wagon!" said Collin.

"Yes, sometimes he can be a handful. I believe we all started on the wrong foot. Allow us to introduce ourselves. My name is Remy and this here fatter brother of mine is Templeton, but me and the lads call him Crackers, for the reason that he is always eating crackers," said Remy, the short rat."

"Very nice to meet you both; my name is Jasper, and these are my companions Eileen and Collin. We come from Cirencester and we aim to get to London as soon as possible," said Jasper.

"You three are bound to London in a time like this?" asked Crackers as he took out a piece of cracker from his inner vest pocket.

"Yes, is that a problem?" asked Collin.

"Well, son, to be frank with you, something is about to happen in London. I'm not sure, but I can feel it in my bones. Come along, we can talk this over a pint of ale, best brew you will not find in any other train."

Remy and Crackers led the rabbits to a secret compartment that opened in the wall with a tunnel that led directly to the kitchen. They quickly ran past several wagons and finally made it to where the rest of Remy's and Crackers friends were.

"Welcome to where we congregate at times and get our food, the human kitchen. When no one is here, it is a buffet for all of us," said Crackers.

Jasper saw that there were several rats carrying and grabbing the food they needed and fleeing back.

They carried bread, cold meats, chicken and refilled in their jugs with whatever beer was available. Just by walking into the kitchen, it would've been a nightmare for any human of seeing so many rodents in one place. The two rats and the rabbits jumped onto the stove and had started to fill their sacks with food.

"Jack and his Pack are a fearsome lot, better not get mixed up with them; us rat's here, we're ugh ... how to put it, nomadic scavengers, we travel all together looking for the best grub!"

"I see how ... adventurous of you, Remy," said Eileen with some hesitation.

"Let's all get back to the wagon where we met, no one will bother us there," said Remy.

Once everyone grabbed a little something from the kitchen they all returned back to the wagon and had their dinner.

"You were saying you escaped from Jack?" asked Remy.

"Well, yes, that is correct. You see, our final stop is in London, and we thought it be easier to take the train. But when we arrived to Kemble we crossed paths with Jack. But thanks to his younger brother, rather round, cheerful fellow, he adores pastries and despises hunting—"

"Are you talking about Kevin?!" asked crackers interrupting Jasper.

"Well, yes! Do you know him?" asked Eileen.

"Know him? Me and that fluffy fox are practically best mates. He also saved me one time from being eaten by his older brother. From time to time we would trade pastries and other delights in private. The rest of my family, with the exception of Crackers of course, does not trust Kevin for being a fox, but me and him have an understanding."

"How delightful," said Eileen.

Remy gives the rabbits and his brother cups of the chef's brown ale. Collin tips his top hat in gratitude.

"So, you were saying, something is about to happen in London?" asked Jasper.

"Aye, that's what me and my family reckon. We have heard talk of humans preparing for an attack. A lot of the city is being fortified and many humans are down under the earth. Never have I ever seen so many humans under the ground, and humans despise rats; it's not safe for us either. Why are you lot going to London?" said Crackers.

"We are going to find my brother."

"London is a big city, lad; many animals live there, good and bad. You have to be careful in who you can trust. Do you have any idea on where you be going?"

"The only lead we have on him was that he was working in a pub called the Phoenix."

"The Phoenix, you say? I've been there a couple times myself; you can find all the London's characters there, you mustn't look faint of heart when you go in there. Out of all the lot in the Phoenix, you must take caution with one."

"Alistair," said Collin.

"Exactly, beware of the falcon," said Remy.

"I do not have the entire story of why he went to the Phoenix. I just want to get him and get out. His name is William, by the way, perhaps you may have heard the name," said Jasper.

"Well, I'll be, your brother is William?! Bill the rabbit?!"

"You know my brother?" asked Jasper with excitement.

"Of course, we do! Bloke is a blessing from Merlin himself! Crackers and me here found ourselves in a pot of trouble, but luckily we were able to make it out alive thanks to him," added Remy.

"He saved you two? What did you do?" asked Jasper.

"We stole food from Alistair. Not very smart on our part. He is the largest bird of prey in London. He is malicious and cruel. He owns the skies, and has other animals working for him on the ground. Including your brother," said Crackers.

"William is working for such a creature?!" asked Jasper.

"It would appear so. He is feared by all animals, including the foxes; many do his dirty work for him. All I can say about your brother is that, when we were brought up in front of Alistair's court, your brother intervened and negotiated our release. We are in his debt," said Remy.

"Why did he help you?" asked Jasper.

"I'm not sure, he had no reason to. Perhaps he felt bad for us. Our punishment would have been death, but I suppose your brother felt the need to intervene," said Crackers as he continued to eat.

"And how such a noble animal could work for a bitter and hostile falcon?" added Crackers.

"Are you alright, Jasper?" asked Collin.

"I am," replied Jasper.

Jasper was confused, he never expected his brother to turn out to be part of a band of animals that prey over others. He wanted to reach London as soon as possible to find his older brother.

"What else must I know about Alistair?" asked Jasper.

"How's your Cockney rhyme and slang?" asked Remy.

"Barely existent," replied Collin.

"No worries, I'll give you a freshen up on the rhyme and slang, you will need it when you meet the hedgehog," said Remy.

"Who is the hedgehog?" asked Eileen.

"Mr. Thorn is his name. Do not let his size fool you, there is not a single fur on his body that makes him good," said Crackers.

"Ok, what else should we know about Alistair?"

"He has an obsession to human wealth, coin, gold, silver, he likes to adorn himself with bright and polished gems and stones. He believes that he is royalty and that he deserves everything. A very impatient bird he is. Sometimes I think he carries the soul of the very evil Mordred himself. He also has a scar over his right eye. It is said that an owl gave him that mark in a fight. Defeated and humiliated, he flew to London to become what he is today, a monster," said Remy.

"What a horrible creature! How can one become so cruel?!" asked Eileen.

"Be careful, as long as you don't get involved in his business, there is a chance you can get out alive," said Remy.

"But, how do I get an audience with him in his court?" asked Jasper!

"Oh, dear me, well, seeing you three are outsiders, hmmm, I reckon if you had something to offer to the Alistair that he could not deny," answered back Crackers.

The rabbits continued to drink their ale as they all thought of what they would need to do when they arrived at the Phoenix.

"And what brings you on this train? It's heading towards London," said Jasper to Remy.

"This train indeed goes to London, but Crackers, the fam' and I are getting off at the village of Didcot and a few in Reading. From Didcot we will be staying in Oxford. We have family there so and we think we will be safe for the time being. Some humans continue to practice magic in private and there are many animals with the gift of speech in Oxford. It is a safe haven for us animals that were blessed by Merlin."

Jasper just sat there and minded to his thoughts. The rest of the trip consisted of Remy teaching Collin how to talk like a natural Cockney.

Remy and Crackers enjoyed the company of the rabbits as they all continued to drink most of the chef's brown ale.

By the time the train arrived at Didcot, the rat pack waited for all the humans to disembark. Jasper, Eileen, and Collin stayed in the train. When Remy and Crackers got off, Remy looked back at his three new friends and yelled.

"The train stops at Paddington Station! For you lot it may be a couple of hours to get to The Phoenix Club. When you get off, head east on Marylebone Road, all the way straight and take a right on Tottenham Road! You will pass several beautiful gardens on your way! Park Square and Fitzroy Square Garden! When you get to Phoenix street, you're there, mate!"

"How would we recognize it?" asked Jasper.

"Trust me! There's no way of missing it! If all goes well with your brother, please do come and visit us in Oxford!"

Remy and Crackers were waiving to the rabbits as the train continued its way to Paddington Station.

"At least we have some direction on how to reach the Phoenix," said Collin.

"I just hope we're not too late."

"Late for what?" asked Eileen.

"My dreams, they still haunt me. I want to get my brother and quickly get on back home to Cirencester."

"Let's sleep up a bit before we get to London."

The three rabbits slept between the boxes. The sound of the train dozed them off to sleep.

15 PADDINGTON STATION

SEPTEMBER 6TH**, 1940.** The train that came from Kemble was arriving at Paddington Station sometime in the evening. As the train descended its speed, its whistle blew notifying its arrival. There was a small window from where the rabbits could see what was happening outside. Jasper peaked through the window and saw hundreds of humans formed outside all cramped together with their luggages.

"Never have I seen these many humans all together at the same time," said Jasper.

"What are they doing out there?" asked Eileen.

"I think they mean to board this train," replied Jasper.

The train finally stopped and the whistle blew again. The rabbits could hear the sound of many human voices talking simultaneously outside. It was hard for them to focus on just one. It was very echoey and loud. The sound of the voices had started to increase on the other side of the slide door they were in.

"Get ready," said Collin. The rabbits had a feeling that something was about to happen. The slide door of the wagon was completely opened and the rabbits were blinded by the light that blazed into the wagon from the outside.

They stayed hidden behind some of the wooden crates that were inside the wagon to observe what would happen. They saw the platform and the people that were on it.

Some sat and stood where they were, others were walking all over the place in a hurry. All of a sudden two humans jumped into the wagon to inspect it. They slowly walked counting how many crates there were and noticed that the barrels were missing.

"Quickly! We must get off before we get caught!" said Jasper.

The rabbits rapidly got off the wagon without being seen from the two humans. They landed near the rail and quietly sat hidden under the train. Eileen was starting to get edgy, as she looked everywhere to see if there would be a good spot to hide. The three of them knew they were momentarily safe, so they stood a little longer to observe their surroundings.

In front of them, they could see several human children all in line wearing gas masks holding tightly to their toys and dolls. Their mothers were next to them all well-dressed crying and tearing up.

Eileen felt sympathy for the humans, for she wanted to somehow comfort them, but did not know how. Collin was amazed by the size of the structure of Paddington Station. He was really mesmerized on how the ceiling was made by metal arches and glass. Jasper was looking for the quickest way to get out, but the whole station was crowded by humans.

Jasper pointed out that behind them there was another platform with what appeared to be sandbags, and there they could take cover. The three of them ran under the train across the middle platform to the adjacent platform and were able to hop on and cover themselves behind the sandbags.

"What do we do know?" asked Collin.

"There! That door is opened! It may be our only way out!" pointed out Eileen.

"Let's go for it!" said Jasper.

"It's too far! Will never get to it without getting noticed!" said Collin.

"There's no other way Collin," said Jasper.

The three of them took a leap of faith and rapidly ran straight towards the opened door. As they ran, the three of them could hear people yelling about rabbits with clothing running through the train station. Many humans stopped where they were going to look at the rabbits. Little children dropped their dolls and toys in awe just to look at them. But people were such in a rush that they did not had the time to pay much attention to them. They thought it was their imagination playing tricks on them.

By the time the rabbits made it through the crowd of people walking back and forth with luggage and children panicking and crying and chaos being everywhere around them, they had finally found themselves outside Paddington Station into the open.

Jasper, Eileen, and Collin were surprised to see the number of humans walking amongst each other on the street. They dressed a bit differently from the ones from Cirencester. The women were very fashionable: hats in different sizes and colours and same with their dresses and skirts. The men had a more uniformed style with jackets and coats, all in blue or in grey. Even the building and architecture was different. The buildings in London were taller and looked older, many of them were made out of brick with little or no space between them. They were also surprised to see the different types of vehicles that were around, they came in all different sizes and colours; the noise, honks of the cars, the repetitive human chatter everywhere and lights were a bit unsettling and side-tracking. There were so many things that drew their attention.

"Welcome to London, boys," said Eileen.

"Oh, as if you know the place around here?" responded Collin.

"We have to stay focused; what were the directions given by Remy?" asked Jasper.

Collin was trying to remember the instructions.

"Let's see, he said to head east of the city, and there would be a couple of gardens, but we should head towards ... "

"Go straight on Marylebone Road and a right on Tottenham Road!" yelled Eileen with excitement. "Let's go, lads!" Eileen was now taking the lead.

"The lass sure is adventurous," said Collin to Jasper.

"Yes, she is," said Jasper.

"Do you think I can get my hands on one of those lovely motor vehicles?" asked Collin.

"Let's not test out our luck, mate," said Jasper.

The rabbits ran straight into the open of Marylebone Road. They figured that the humans would be so busy preparing for their war, that who would bat an eye on three rabbits in the middle of London. As they ran, they saw several groupings of soldiers getting together in different places, there were different military vehicles roaming around the city. In specific spots there were soldiers with long cannons pointing up towards the sky; other humans that were not soldiers were grouping up into houses and apartments. They did not see any open markets like the ones in Cirencester, all the shops that sold food seemed to be cleaned out or packed with other humans running amok amongst themselves.

"What in the world is happening here?" asked Eileen.

"I feel that my dreams are slowly creeping into reality. Let's just focus on getting my brother and getting back to the station!"

After forty minutes of running non-stop on Marylebone Road, they were almost on Tottenham Road. As they were running, Eileen could not help to notice that there were being followed by several stray cats on rooftops and they were observing them from above. She pointed this out to Jasper and Collin. They decided not to pay attention to them and to continue onward towards their destination. They finally stopped on a street corner and looked towards the street signs.

"Great! We are now on Tottenham Road!" panted Jasper.

"C'mon on, lads, we must keep up the pace!" said Eileen.

"Who would know that this lass could outrun us," said Collin.

They were now running down towards Tottenham Road as quickly as they could. They could see planes flying overhead them. They were fascinated on how different things were in London and how peaceful it can be living in the English countryside compared to the concrete jungle they were in.

They have now been running for another forty minutes down Tottenham road and the night was approaching. As the darkness of the night overcame London, there were less humans on the streets.

Eileen looked over her shoulder and could see that the cats were still following them.

"Where is this place?" asked Collin.

"It must be a little bit further. We haven't passed Phoenix Street yet. We must press on," said Jasper.

They were now getting tired and they could hear that the clouds were starting to rumble.

"It looks like it's going to rain, boys," said Eileen.

"We need to find this place before it starts pouring," replied Jasper.

For another fifteen minutes they continued to press on. And then, it started to rain. They saw how the rainwater carried all the dirt from streets straight to the gutter. In the water that was being directed to the gutters they could see posters of propaganda saying things like 'Air Raids', 'Find Your Shelter' and 'Service for Your Country and King'.

"What do you think these posters mean, eh, Jasper?"

"I'm not sure. Collin, but I feel in my gut that something is a brewing."

As the floor was starting to get more wet, Collin slipped and bruised his knee.

"Collin! Eileen, hold on!" cried Jasper.

Jasper quickly went back to help Collin get back up.

"Are you alright?!"

"I'm fine, just a wee tumble. Nothing to get all worked up for. But it appears that my lucky tobacco came out from my pocket, and now it's all wet. Oh, dear, what a shame!"

"Well, there will be more tobacco and pints once we get back home to Cirencester," said Jasper as he patted down Collin's jacket. It was a bit dirty.

"Hey you two, look up," said Eileen.

As Jasper and Collin looked up, they could see the rain drizzling down their faces. Upon their sight they read the street sign 'Phoenix Street'. And right on the corner where they were standing, they saw a wooden sign pointing out from the building with the letter 'The Phoenix Club'. On the same wooden sign there was a painting of a beautiful Phoenix adorned with fire and gold. The detail was outstanding. It almost felt as if it would pop out and fly.

"We bloody did it! We arrived at the Phoenix! We're here!" cried Collin.

The three rabbits jumped in the air with much joy and emotion in their hearts knowing that they arrived at their location. Beating all odds against them, Jasper could feel that he was getting closer and closer to his brother William.

Just by standing outside the door, they noticed that that building seemed to be abandoned. There were no lights coming from the inside. The main door seemed old and dirty. However, next to the big door there was a smaller door that seemed to be in better conditions. Eileen put her ear against the door and she could hear a very faint sound of movement coming from the inside.

"Are we on the right street?" asked Collin.

"We must be," answered Jasper.

"So, what now? What's the plan?" asked Eileen.

"Yea Jasper, how do we find your brother? Do we knock on the door? You think they'll just let us come inside?" asked Collin.

"We'll find out, but we may have something that may grant us passage," said Jasper. And right before he could continue on what he was about to say, the group of feral cats that were following them appeared behind them.

"What have we here, eh?" From above came down a gang of street cats surrounding the three rabbits.

"Oh, no!" said Eileen softly.

"We've been watching you three rabbits running all over the place, straight from Paddington Station. What brings you to Phoenix on this cold and rainy night?" asked one cat, whose fur was completely black. The moonlight reflected his shiny fur.

Eileen starts to silently tiptoe to the smaller door.

"We have business in the Phoenix," said Jasper.

"Business, you say? What type of business do you have?" asked the black cat.

Jasper did not have a plan 'b' for this situation; in fact he wasn't prepared to be confronted by a gang of cats at all.

"I asked you, rabbit, what is your business here?" The cat and his feline companions were slowly approaching the three. The rabbits could feel their penetrating eyes on them and could see that their claws were coming out. In any minute now they would pounce and rip the rabbits to shreds.

Eileen was against the door of the Phoenix knocking very fast. She knocked and knocked until someone would open from the inside.

"We're not looking for trouble," said Collin.

"Oh, no trouble here, maybe for you three. Boys, it

looks like we have our dinner!" And right before the cats would attack the door opened.

"Is that you Riff-Raff?" Out from the door came out walking a sturdy hedgehog wearing a green vest and dark sunglasses.

"Ehm, why-why, yes, Mr. Thorn, it is me," said the black cat.

"Come here, you, it is you innit!" The hedgehog was grabbing the cat by its collar. "My eyesight might not be as good as before, but I can sure smell trouble! You ain't starting no barney rubble out here are, ya?" asked Mr. Thorn.

"No, no, no, Mr. Thorn, no barney rubble here," replied Riff-Raff in a nervous matter.

"Good, because we don't like trouble around 'ere". Matter of fact, where's my bees and honey? Eh?" Mr. Thorn pulled Riff-Raff's collar even more. None of the cats intervened.

"I'm still working on it, Mr. Thorn!" Riff-Raff was now shaking.

"If I see you around these parts again without what's owed, you'll be dealing with Alistair him very self, see! Now scram!"

Mr. Thorn was not an animal you wanted to cross either. And the gang of cats went running away.

"You lot! Yeah, you three, inside, I'm getting soaked," said Mr. Thorn to Jasper, Eileen, and Collin.

And the three rabbits were finally inside the Phoenix Club.

16 THE PHOENIX CLUB

ONCE INSIDE THE INFAMOUS Phoenix Club, the three rabbits walked in mesmerized by what they saw. The entire club was empty of humans but filled with animals of all types. There were herons, badgers, foxes, rats, mice, squirrels, all different types of characters and they were having a very loud party. Some were dressed very elegantly with monocles and golden chain watches. But the look on their faces was unfriendly. Others were dressed very rundown and looked aggressive and menacing.

There was smoking, gambling, drinking and there were a couple of brawls or more. Empty pints would be flying across the room and tables would be broken along with the chairs in quarrel. It looked more like a saloon than a club.

"Now, lemme introduce myself," said Mr. Thorn as he cleared his throat and tugged forward his vest. "My name is Mr. Thorn. Now, let's get one thing straight 'ere, I don't know you, and you better tell me what business you have 'ere at the Phoenix."

Before Jasper or Eileen could answer, Collin quickly remembered that Crackers had taught him how to speak and understand Cockney rhyme and slang. He also remembered that he was warned to be careful when they came across a hedgehog that worked in the Phoenix.

The three rabbits were so astonished with the Phoenix that they were utterly speechless. Never in a thousand years would they have seen something like this back home in Cirencester.

"Look 'ere! I'm this close of kicking you lot back into the rain if I don't get names and business this instant!"

"Forgive our rudeness, Mr. Thorn, my name is Collin, at your service." Collin bows and lifts his top hat. "And these are my friends, Mr. Jasper and Miss Eileen. We would like to enter the Phoenix."

"What would the likes of you three be wanting to do in the Phoenix?" asks Mr. Thorn as he laughs at the rabbits. "The three of you are in the wrong place, get lost!"

"We've come very far, Mr. Thorn, we come from Cirencester!" said Collin in a moment of despair.

Jasper and Eileen are concern if whether it was a good idea that Collin have mentioned they were from Cirencester.

"I don't Adam and Eve it, you three are from that small village?" said Mr. Thorn surprisingly.

"Why certainly, Mr. Thorn. You see, we ran away from our home and we heard that the best way to start a new life in London was look for The Phoenix," said Jasper. He tried his very best to make a convincing lie.

"I see, you came all the way from the west country to London, to come here?" asked Mr. Thorn in a curious manner.

"Of course!" said Collin. "I see you and your guests here are having a proper knees up event. May we come in?" asked Collin.

"Not so fast, you cheeky rabbit, not anyone is allowed into the Phoenix, they first got to get through me. You see them animals back there? We have some of the most notorious and distinguished guests of all of London. We got thieves, thugs, muggers, robbers, business animals, proper characters if I say so! I do admit some of them need some bob hope, but it is what it is," said Mr. Thorn.

When Eileen heard the words 'distinguished' and 'notorious', she could not help seeing the behavior of some of these animals, they were acting a bit savage-like. There facial expressions were not comforting, some were completely sloshed, some had marks and scars on their faces and arms. They were aggressive and rude. Back in Cirencester she had never seen animals act in such a way. She wondered whatever could have made them act like that.

"Look, mate, you gotta get your brass tacks straight; if you don't have any bread and honey or something of value worth my time or the bosses, you're not comin in," said Mr. Thorn.

"Right, well, we have something that may be of your interest," said Jasper.

"Well, spill the beans! What is it?" Mr. Thorn's patience was growing thin.

Jasper puts his hand in his sack to take out the stone given to him by his mother before they left Cirencester. It was raveled in a cloth. He hands it to Mr. Thorn. As the hedgehogs unravels the cloth, he is stupefied with what he sees.

"A rock? Are you mad? A bloody pebble?"

"Not any stone, Mr. Thorn, it's a magic stone, a druid stone in fact," said Jasper.

"Magic and druid, you say? You better not be having a bubble bath. How does this work?"

"Very simple, whenever someone is lying the stone turns a bright blue. It never fails," added Collin.

"Is that so? Hand it over, let's take a gander." Mr. Thorn holds the stone against the light to have a better look at it. "Well, let's see if your right?! But if you're lying you and your friends will regret ever coming here."

Mr. Thorn starts calling some from the crowd.

"Oi! Oi! Oscar! Yes, yes, you! Get over here!" A red cat comes over and asks Mr. Thorn what's the problem.

"I'm going to ask you a question, and I don't want lies! I'll know if you're lying." The cat nods in agreement.

"Have you paid your tab yet?" The cat looks at the rabbits and then back to Mr. Thorn. He starts to get a little nervous.

"I asked you a question, Oscar, have you or have you not paid your tab?"

"Why, yes of course, Mr. Thorn. I wouldn't be here in the Phoenix if I didn't. I wouldn't dare cheat you or the boss."

Mr. Thorn places the stone in front of his very eyes, and gives it a butcher's hook, very carefully. And the stone went bright blue.

"You cheeky bugger, I know you haven't paid! And yet you try to take me as fool!"

Before Oscar could say anything, Mr. Thorn opens the door and kicks him right out into the rain.

"So, what do you think, Mr. Thorn?" asked Collin.

"I think we have ourselves a proper transaction. You three are welcomed ... for now ... into London's finest establishment." Mr. Thorn walks the three rabbits in. "Let's have a ball and chalk inside."

"Thank you, Mr. Thorn," said Eileen in her sweetest voice. Mr. Thorn stopped walking and turned his back.

"Oh, dearest me, I didn't see you, look at that beautiful boat race," said Mr. Thorn to Eileen.

"Pardon?" asked Eileen.

"Your face dear, a beautiful face, better stick close to one of these gents here, place may be too rough on you."

"Thank you, Mr. Thorn, but I can take care of myself perfectly fine," replied Eileen.

Mr. Thorn silently chuckled. "Sure you can lass, sure you can."

17 GINGER THE RED SQUIRREL

THE THREE RABBITS were being guided by Mr. Thorn into the Phoenix. The three of them observed their surroundings. They noticed that some of the other animals were looking at them with unwelcoming faces as they walked in with Mr. Thorn.

There were various types of gambling, games like blackjack, craps, and roulette. On the tables there were piles of gold, silver, diamonds, and other exotic metals, stones, and gems. Jasper would closely observe the eyes of the players and they were filled with greed. Somehow this place was bringing out the worse in them.

"Where do you think my brother could be?" asked Jasper to Eileen.

"I don't know, but we have to find him and get out. Some of the other animals are staring at us," said Eileen.

"I know, it doesn't feel good to be in here," said Jasper.

Mr. Thorn led them to the entertainment section of the club. There were several guests seated in front of a stage.

"I would like to further inquire about this stone, I need to speak with one of you in private," said Mr. Thorn.

"You can speak with me, Mr. Thorn," said Collin. Jasper did not expect Collin to volunteer himself.

"Great, meanwhile the two of you please enjoy the show," chuckles Mr. Thorn. "Don't worry, I'll bring your friend right back, just a couple of questions, that's all."

"Jasper, I'll be right back," said Collin.

"You take care," said Jasper.

Jasper and Collin look at each other. They did not say anything, but they both knew something was not right.

"Look over there, it looks like the show is about to begin." Eileen pointed to the stage that had a very beautiful and bright red curtain. Next to the stage was a small piano where a badger was playing.

"While we wait for Collin we might as well stay put. But keep your eyes open," said Jasper. As the lights started to dim, up came a mouse dressed very elegant and very sharp. He had a tuxedo, two gold teeth and his hair was combed very fashionably to the sides.

"Ladies and Gentlemen, it is my pleasure to introduce, the one, the only... Ginger Squirrel!" The red curtains rise and on the stage is a gorgeous red squirrel sitting on a swing and holding a cane, and behind her was a live big band.

The animals that were watching the show went wild! They were clapping, cheering, standing up and banging the tables with their paws.

She was wearing a very shiny and provocative red dress that sparkled and reflected with the stage lights. The live band started out with a smooth tune that the piano followed. When the music lowered, the stage lights dimmed down, and the spotlight was on her. She started to sing softly.

Jasper could not keep his eyes off her, he saw elegance and grace in her performance. She walked with the tempo of the music across the stage flirting with the audience. From the public you could hear some of the animals whistling and cheering back at her. Eileen was not really impressed with what she was seeing. In a part of the performance, Ginger snaps her finger and that is when the big band starts playing a more of an upbeat and faster rhythm and the lights really brightens up the stage.

The sound of the drums and the trumpets evokes a sense of an explosive euphoria. Ginger is now swinging from the swing, singing from the top of her lungs, and the crowd goes wild. Jasper is watching with his mouth opened and Eileen is next to him pouting.

Ginger jumps from the swing and is now singing on the tables of some of the audience members. She jumps on the table where Jasper and Eileen are sitting and gives him a wink. Jasper claps loudly and she jumps to another table. Eileen is pouting even more and gives a mean stare to Jasper.

By the time the song is reaching its finale, Ginger makes her way onto the stage and bows in front of the crowd. The audience and Jasper give her a standing ovation, they're throwing roses, hats, coats and even pieces of gold and silver as the curtains fall.

"What an amazing show? What did you think, Eileen?"

"It was ... alright, I suppose," said Eileen unimpressed.

Jasper chuckles on how Eileen is reacting. As the audience starts to calm themselves down, most of them get up from their tables and head back to gamble or go to the bar. Across from where Jasper and Eileen are sitting, near the piano, Ginger is thanking the piano player for playing so well. She is now wearing a coat over her red dress and walks over to where the rabbits are.

"Well, what do we have here?" asked Ginger.

"A pair of nobodies," said Eileen.

Ginger slightly wraps her tail around Jasper and sits with them at their table.

"Nice to meet a pair of nobodies. I have an eye for new faces, and you two don't look like the typical customers. In fact, neither of you look like you belong here," said Ginger.

"We don't tend to stay too long, we're just looking for someone. Great show by the way," said Jasper.

"Thank you, darling, very kind of you. Well, I hope you find who you are looking for. Who might it be, if you don't mind me asking?"

"We would rather if that be private, thank you, Ginger," said Eileen.

"Alright, your business is your business. But this is fair warning, the animal that owns this place, Alistair; be careful. Let me know if there's anything I can do to help." Ginger gets up from the table and starts to leave.

"Wait, maybe there is," said Jasper.

"No! Don't tell her why we're here! We don't know if we can trust her!" said Eileen. But Jasper starts to ask anyway.

"How long have you been here? In the Phoenix Club?" asks Jasper.

"I've been here far too long, rabbit," answered Ginger.

"I don't know if I can trust you or not, but I have this weird feeling that I can. Have you ever seen another rabbit in this place, with blur fur, black eyes and with the name of William?" asked Jasper.

"Jasper, hush! You're saying to much!" says Eileen.

"Who are you exactly?" asked Ginger cautiously as she leans towards Jasper.

"Who am I is of no importance. I just need to know if William is here. We have come from a very far place and have done the impossible to be here," says Jasper.

"Listen to me, rabbit, I do not know who you are, but you should be very careful coming into the Phoenix and saying that name. Now, it's obvious you two are not from here and do not belong here! I strongly advise the both of you leave before it's too late," said Ginger. She got up and started to walk again.

"We are looking for my brother, William, and we come from Cirencester. You can understand that we cannot just get up and leave," said Jasper.

Ginger stops again from walking away. She turns very slowly and takes a look at Jasper. She sits back at the table where the rabbits are.

"As I said, we've come this far, and we are not leaving London empty-handed," added Jasper.

Ginger stares at both of them, mainly at Jasper. She takes in a deep breath.

"What if I knew him? What then? What could a couple of rabbits do? Do you know who Alistair is?"

"Wait, what is going on? Do you know his brother?" asked Eileen.

"How can I not! Everyone knows William here!" Ginger is trying not to get emotional. "I'm the reason why he came here!" She tries to control herself and not bring too much attention upon herself.

"What?" Jasper slightly leans back trying to make sense of what he just heard. "Who are you? Tell me where he is, Ginger, I beg of you," pleaded Jasper.

"I've said too much already; besides, the way to get to your brother is through Alistair," replied Ginger.

"Then, where is Alistair? Tell me, Ginger."

"No, I cannot. Please, the both of you have to leave before it's too late. If he finds who you are and what you are doing here you will never leave this place!"

"Either way we cannot leave, we came with another friend," said Jasper.

"Where is your friend?!" asked Ginger.

"He and Mr. Thorn are speaking in private."

"You two have to leave this place right now! You cannot trust Mr. Thorn! I fear there's no hope for him," said Ginger.

"Is he in trouble?" asked Eileen with a worry.

"There's no time, quickly grab your things! I'll walk you to the door," said Ginger in a hurry.

"We can't leave! What did you mean when you said you're the reason why my brother is here?"

In that moment, before Ginger could get up, she felt a tap on her shoulder from the back. It was Mr. Thorn.

"Take a seat, love, you seem to be in a hurry," said Mr. Thorn as he took out the biggest cigar they had ever seen from his vest and lit it. He grabbed a chair a sat with them.

Ginger did as she was told and sat there frozen with her eyes wide open and with her heart beating rapidly.

Mr. Thorn sat next to Ginger and smiled at the rabbits. Jasper asked him where Collin was, but Mr. Thorn did not answer his question.

"Ran away from home, did you, now?" asked Mr. Thorn as he smoked his oversize cigar. Before Jasper could say anything, Mr. Thorn interrupted him saying that Alistair wanted to see him. And if he refused it would end very badly for him and for Eileen.

"Thorn, they mean no harm, there just a pair of harmless rabbits," said Ginger.

"Alistair will decide whether they're harmless or not. If I were you, Ginger, I'd be very careful; just remember what happened the last time," said Mr. Thorn as he chuckled. "Come on, you two, better not keep the boss waiting," said Mr. Thorn.

The rabbits stood up and followed Mr. Thorn. Ginger sat there by herself at the table as she watched them get up and leave.

18 ALISTAIR THE FALCON

MR. THORN WAS WALKING in front of Jasper and Eileen. He was guiding them through a corridor that had dimmed lights. The walls and floor were made of old oak and, in every step, you could hear the creaking floor. The ambiance was very unsettling.

"Where is our friend, Mr. Thorn?" asked Jasper now with a more affirmative tone.

"Young master Collin had many tales to tell. Such a pleasant young rabbit to chat with," replied Mr. Thorn.

"And where exactly is he now?" asked Eileen.

"Why, in a moment you shall see him," said Mr. Thorn.

Jasper was trying to find the relation between his brother, Ginger, and Alistair. He was also thinking about Ginger's warning and how she wanted them to leave the Phoenix immediately.

"Tell me, what have you heard about Alistair?" asked Mr. Thorn to the rabbits.

"Well, we have heard that he is a very important falcon here in London. He likes to be surrounded by shiny objects, objects that humans value," replied Jasper.

"What else have you heard?"

"It is best not to anger him," replied Eileen.

"There is one thing that really bothers Alistair. Do you know what that is? I will tell you. Animals coming into his house and having secrets. If one has secrets, it is because one is hiding something, would you agree?" asked Mr. Thorn.

"I would guess so," replied Jasper.

"When I know an animal has secrets, the first thought that comes to my mind is that they want to take something from Alistair, and that is something that he does not forgive."

Jasper and Eileen are thinking about why Mr. Thorn is telling them all this; they feel something is happening here.

"There was an animal that used to work for us, he seemed trustworthy at the beginning, but it turned out he had secrets and wanted to take away something that belonged to him."

The three of them arrive at the end of the corridor. Jasper is getting nervous. He does not like the way Mr. Thorn is talking to them. Mr. Thorn slightly opens the door, and before opening it completely, he turns back and looks directly into Jasper's eye.

"I believe you know who I speak of. I reckon I can guess what your business is with Alistair. I would like to know what it is?

Jasper and Eileen stand very still, and neither gives Mr. Thorn a response.

"As I told you both before, my sight may not be the best, but I can always smell foul play."

Mr. Thorn opens the door wide open to the next room. He takes a step to stand behind the rabbits. They enter a room with a circular shape that looks like a dome. The room was black and dark. The only light seen in the room was the moonlight that entered through a large hole in the ceiling. At the very back of the room, within the shadows, Jasper and Eileen could get a glimpse of what appeared to be a throne. At the base of the throne, they could see a large claw surrounded by a pile of gold and silver.

"Alistair!" Jasper whispers his name.

"Go on; he won't bite! Have your audience with Alistair!" Mr. Thorn from behind shoves Jasper and Eileen into the room. They both tumble and trip inside, and Mr. Thorn shuts the door and laughs horridly. Both of their hearts are pounding. Jasper looks around the room, trying to find a way to escape, but the only way out is above them.

"Come into the light, don't be timid," said Alistair in a low and raspy voice as he remained sitting in the shadows. Jasper and Eileen take small steps right onto the edge of where the moonlight is hitting the floor.

"Tell me, what business brings a nice pair of rabbits as yourselves to the Phoenix?" asked Alistair.

Eileen is silent.

"We have fled our home for a new life," said Jasper in a nervous tone. He repeats the same lie he told Mr. Thorn.

There is no response from Alistair. Silence stains in the air.

"You see, we have come from afar. Our journey has been long and tiring. We have seen a new world of which we did not know existed. But when the tales of Alistair the Falcon reached our small and peaceful village, I could not resist coming here. I had to leave my monotonous and colourless life and gaze upon the shining and magnificent falcon that so many fear and respect." Jasper tried to speak with more confidence, but his voice kept breaking.

"I once lived in a peaceful village, you know? Filled with magic and wonder, tell me, does the name Socrates mean anything to you?" asked Alistair.

Jasper and Eileen looked at each other, wondering what lie would they say. "We've heard that name before, but we have no relation to him," replied Jasper, quickly wanting to change the subject.

From where Jasper and Eileen were standing, they could see Alistair slowly opening his eyes. They had a dark golden colour that mesmerized you, that drew you in and made you feel inconsequential. Neither of them had ever seen eyes that were so yellow and aureate.

Straight from the shadows, Alistair aggressively thrusts from his throne and flies fearlessly toward Jasper and Eileen. He stops and lands in front of them with his wings spread out, imposing his colossal stature. Both rabbits observe the large falcon; he wears shiny and expensive accessories, gold and silver chains around his neck. His claws were covered in gold paint. Even his feathers had a tone of gold. He lowers his wings and starts to walk around the rabbits making them walk slowly into the middle of the room.

"I am curious to know what stories you have heard about me, rabbit?" asked Alistair. Jasper was thinking of a response that would be fit for Alistair.

"I am filled with contentment to finally set my eyes upon an animal that resembles an actual phoenix. You are adorned with richness, fit for a falcon of your force. We have heard of your reputation, Alistair, of how you rule the skies in London; animals here respect you, fear you, no one dares to defy you. You are an inspiration to all those who aspire to be powerful and respected."

Alistair lowers his head and stares right into the eyes of Jasper. "You flatter me well, rabbit, even though you do not seem the type who seeks power. What is your name and where do you come from? If you do not mind me asking," said Alistair.

"I come ... come from a small village with a beautiful forest with tall trees, from where the druids used to roam, where the wisest gather. They call me the Friend of rats, the Deceiver of foxes, and the Confronter of humans!" said Jasper.

"Confronter of humans? Deceiver of foxes? You must be very brave for a little rabbit; you must have no fear in you," said Alistair, as he started to straighten his back slowly.

"We have endured much, and I am not easily frightened," replied Jasper nervously.

"Then, why do you tremble?! Do not lie to me! I can smell the terror inside of you. You dare masquerade yourself in my room with such titles, rabbit! A charlatan before me!"

"We do not lie, great Alistair, for we would never insult you by concealing secrets from you, for we know that would be most unfavourable for us," intervened Eileen, trying to be confident.

"Do you know what happens to those who slander in front of me, young rabbit?" asked Alistair as his eyes pierced Eileen's eyes. "They never see the light of day," said Alistair.

"We wish to join your ranks, Alistair, that is if you find us worthy, of course," said Jasper as he nervously cleared his throat.

"And why would I let two country rabbits join me? How do I know you are not lying?! How do I know I can trust you?! How do I know if you are not hiding anything from me?!" asked Alistair as his tone increased.

"We are not hiding from you, Alistair!" cried Jasper

"Did Socrates send you?! Tell me now, rabbit!" Alistair is starting to become aggressive. But Jasper and Eileen cannot answer as they are struck with fear.

"I have an idea; let's play a game, shall we?" Alistair turns sideways and points with his wing at the right side of his throne. Slowly emerging from the shadows and walking towards the light is Collin — all beaten up and in chains. Both Jasper and Eileen are shocked to see their friend injured. They make sure not to make any sudden movements.

"I was thinking of cutting him up tonight, right where you two are standing, actually. I'm sure you won't oppose," said Alistair.

Jasper and Eileen gaze in shock and sadness at the condition their friend Collin is in. "What has he done to deserve such a punishment?" asked Eileen.

"So, you do oppose?" replied Alistair.

Collin looks at Eileen and Jasper and shakes his head. He doesn't want either of them to say anything.

"If you could give me a good reason why I should spare him, I will consider it," said Alistair.

He glided to where Collin was, grabbed him with his claws, and flew right back to where the rabbits were.

"Well, anything to say? Jasper?" asked Alistair.

"Let him live, and he could proof his value," replied Jasper impatiently.

"I disagree, rabbit," said Alistair. He quickly pushes Collin's body down onto the floor with his claw.

"Collin!" yelled Jasper. Alistair releases Collin and looks at Jasper.

"You rabbits take me as a fool! Even though hearing you was very amusing! Blinded by your courage, there is one more surprise for you!"

From the left side of Alistair's throne comes walking another rabbit into the light. He slowly made his appearance and his blue fur shined ever so brightly with the moonlight; he too was in a very bad shape, a lot worse than Collin. His arms and legs were chained and had minimal movement. He came walking at a very slow speed; the sound of the chains rattling was loud.

"William?" Jasper whispered his name. "William, is that you?"

There was no response from his brother, and Alistair laughed amusingly at the situation.

"How delightful to be present in the reunification of brothers. Wouldn't you say, Jasper?" asked Alistair.

"What have you done to my brother, you ungodly creature?!" asked Jasper.

"This is what happens to those who come into my house and try to steal what belongs to me. All of you are bound to me!"

"I can't believe you came all the way out here, little brother," said William. Re-hearing the voice of his brother was a conflict of emotions for Jasper. He was happy to finally see him after all this time, but at the same time, he was angry that he had left.

"Jasper, leave this unholy place, leave while you can!" said Collin.

"Silence, the both of you! Now, Jasper, let's play another game, shall we?" said Alistair. He commands his brother to come forward. Alistair smiles as he sees William walking in pain. Jasper is now closer to his brother than he has ever been in years. Alistair spreads out his wings; he grabs both Collin and William with his claws by their heads and flies straight up.

"This will be your punishment for your lies, Jasper! You have to choose one, who do you save, your brother who you have travelled all this way to save, or your friend? Who will have their dance with death?" asked Alistair as he flapped his wings into the air. "You have to choose wisely, Jasper, because, I assure you, one will not survive the drop!"

William and Collin were both screaming down at Jasper and Eileen to make a run for it, that they should escape.

"Make a decision now, Jasper, or I will drop them both! Do not test me, vermin!" reassured Alistair.

"Jasper, you have to make a decision now!" said Eileen.

All the screaming, yelling, and commotion coming from William, Collin, Eileen, and Alistair made Jasper nauseous. He knew he had to make a decision quickly because he would have neither his friend nor his brother in a few moments. They all knew the risks of coming to London, the different outcomes and possibilities that could happen. But it never occurred to him that he would be choosing between the life of his brother or friend.

"Well, what will it be, Jasper?!" asked Alistair.

"I have a better offer, Alistair," said Jasper.

"You wish to strike a deal? Interesting, what bargaining power may you have in your position?" asked Alistair.

"Take me and release William and Collin," said Jasper.

"No, Jasper," said Eileen in a low voice.

"Not enough, foolish rabbit. I could take the lives of the four of you, if I pleased," replied Alistair as he laughed. While he was in the sky, he could hear the sirens of the city had started going off. His grip was growing tighter as he heard the loud noise. The sounds made Alistair uneasy, paranoid and distracted him. From the ground, the rabbits saw how Alistair was diverted to what was around him. He finally flew down, still holding onto the heads of William and Collin.

"Thorn! Thorn! Come out here!" cried Alistair.

Mr. Thorn, with another group of thug-looking animals, comes into the room.

"Take these rabbits and throw them into confinement! Their fate will be settled tomorrow evening! The ruckus from outside disturbs me; it doesn't allow me to think clearly!" shouted Alistair.

"As you say, Alistair, as you say. Also, I feel obliged to inform you that some of the regulars are leaving town, they fear trouble may be approaching. I suggest we do the same," said Mr. Thorn.

"Do as you're told, Thorn, and take them to confinement! Fear does not commandeer my decisions!" cried Alistair

"Yes, sir," responded Mr. Thorn as he and his thugs shackled the four rabbits and took them towards a cell.

19 WILLIAM

MR. THORN UNCHAINED the shackles that William and Collin bore, and the four rabbits were thrown into a cell. The room was not very spacious, the floor was dirty, and the bars were covered in rust. The whole place was dark, damp, and filthy. Collin was lying in the corner of the cell, trying to recover from the beating Alistair's thugs gave him.

"Collin! What did they do to you?! Let me look at your wounds!" said Eileen as she kneeled to examine his bruises and wounds, but Collin insisted that he was fine.

As Eileen was attending Collin, Jasper and William had an awkward silence. They both observed each other, thinking of all the time that had passed without seeing each other. Jasper was at a loss for words, yearning to find the right things to say at that moment. He stared into the beaten face of his brother, disappointed in him that he left his home to end up in a place like the Phoenix.

"Well? William?" asked Jasper.

"Well, what, little brother?" replied William.

"Do you have the slightest clue of the pain and suffering you have caused mum and me? You left us. You left without saying goodbye to me, your younger brother! You were everything to me, and you have nothing to say!"

Jasper was trying very hard to hold his tears back. He was infuriated with himself because he felt useless.

"And now, I have jeopardized the lives of my friends to save yours!" added Jasper.

Eileen and Collin sat silently in a corner, watching Jasper let all emotions come out.

"Well, William? Do you have anything to say? Do you? Tell me, was it worth it? Did you finally find what you were looking for?"

Jasper was trying to control his breathing, but he was overflowing with adrenaline.

Aching in pain as he was, William stood on his two feet. "I'm sorry, I am sorry that I made you leave mum and come all this way for me. Hurting you both was the last thing I ever wanted to do. I did not intend to stay this long in London! But you must listen to me! Yes, my intentions were vain and foolish at the beginning! But something happened that delayed my return. There is something bigger you must understand!" said William.

Jasper looks confused.

"What do you mean, something bigger? Mum told me about your obsession with learning magic! That was your main reason!" yelled Jasper.

"I came here for a specific reason; I came to bring someone back that does not belong here. She has been held here against her will, imprisoned in this place. I did crave adventure, but leaving you and mum forever and not coming back was never part of the plan," said William.

"Who do you speak of?" asked Jasper.

"The very same person that taught our mother magic," replied William.

Jasper stands frozen for a moment as he tries to make sense of what his brother just said.

"The druid you went looking for in the forest and never found? Brother, I need you to explain in detail what you speak," said Jasper.

"I will, brother, but let me rest and let us think how to get out of here. I don't want to stay here any longer," replied William softly as he slowly laid on the floor dozed off.

While William and Collin rested and recovered, Jasper and Eileen were thinking of how to escape. They tried kicking open the cell door. They looked around to see if something was lying on the floor that they could use to break free, but there was nothing. They noticed there were more cells, but they were all empty. Just looking at them evoked an eerie feeling, and they thought to themselves, what kind of animal would imprison other animals and what drove Alistair to be so cruel? Jasper and Eileen were now tired of trying to find a way out, for it was futile.

"What do we do now?" asked Eileen.

"I don't know. I'm sorry I brought you two here to this place. I should have stopped you both," said Jasper with sad eyes.

"Don't apologize. It's not your fault ... "

Before Eileen could continue, William was starting to awaken and moan at the same time. Jasper walks to his brother.

"William, how do we get out of here? There must be some way out," asked Jasper impatiently.

"I'm afraid not, little brother. Mr. Thorn personally had these cells made to be unbreakable," replied William, still in some agony.

"Are we to just sit here until Alistair decides what to do with us?" asked Eileen.

"I hate to say it, but yes." William sits up. "We might need to improvise when Thorn comes and gets us," said William.

"Great, all this way to end up in a cell, I'm sure mum would be happy to see us right about now," snarked Jasper to his brother.

"Don't blame me for your decision in coming here, Jasper!" responded William.

Eileen just stood to the side, watching the brothers argue.

"Well, what was I supposed to do? I saw you in my dreams, William! I saw this whole city in flames! I saw the destruction that will come upon this place. I came here to bring you back home before it would be too late, and now I fear that it may never happen!" Jasper turns around and starts hitting the cell door in desperation.

"You dreamt of me, little brother?" William was touched to hear this. "Perhaps magic runs in you as well as mum."

"I don't care about magic! I care about us! About home!" Jasper continues to be distressed.

"Going back home, to the beautiful rolling hills of the west country, to see the warm smile of mum's face again and seeing all of our friends in the forest, living freely is all I want," replied William calmly.

"Then help us find an escape!" said Jasper.

"I will, but first, you need to know why I came here, little brother, for I am not the monster you think I am." At that moment, William shared the truth with Jasper.

Not too long ago, Alistair used to live in Cirencester. He was one of the few falcons that lived there. Socrates kept a close eye on him for many years, for he dwelled obsessively in dark magic. He learned forbidden spells and summons, for he wanted to become human and turn himself into a warlock. He was against the ideals of the Covenant and wanted to be stronger than them. On one stormy night, deep in the forest, Alistair successfully summoned an evil spirit that would grant him his wish to become human. He summoned the spirit of Balor the Smiter, a giant cyclops. He carries a spear but be aware of his eye, for it shoots a beam that obliterates everything. He is an evil spirit, filled with maliciousness straight to its core. Balor was willing to grant Alistair's wish in return for his loyalty and devotion. They both agreed, and Alistair was turned into a human. The process was painful but quick. Though he only enjoyed it for a short time for it was Socrates and Maeve who stopped him.

There was a duel between Maeve and the human form of Alistair. Maeve was stronger and defeated Alistair quickly. When Maeve was about to destroy him, Alistair summoned Balor again and pleaded for his help. Balor saw Maeve and recognized that she was a follower of Merlin. Detesting what he saw, Balor decided to turn Maeve into a red squirrel, taking away most of her magic. But that wasn't the end of things. Balor was discontented with Alistair for being so weak. He expected more from him. Unable to defeat Maeve, Balor decided Alistair did not deserve his human form and was turned back into a falcon. After this, Balor simply vanished.

At this moment, Socrates decided it was his turn to intervene and fight against Alistair. Socrates scars Alistair in the right eye, causing him great pain. Alistair knew that victory was unattainable and thought of the alternative. Instead of continuing the fight, he flies towards the squirrel form of Maeve, grabs her, and flees. Socrates tries to stop Alistair from flying away but cannot catch him. Ever since, Alistair has had Maeve imprisoned in the Phoenix, making her do silly performances.

"So, the squirrel that performs in the Phoenix is the druid that was kidnapped?" asked Jasper.

"Yes! When did you meet her?!" asked William.

"We walked into her performance when we entered the Phoenix, and she approached us right after. The moment she knew I was your brother and was looking for you, she told me to quickly leave and not return. But before we could do anything, Mr. Thorn appeared, took us to see Alistair, and now we're here," replied Jasper.

"We have to be careful with Mr. Thorn, he may have poor eyesight, but he sees everything that happens in the Phoenix. Alistair has poor Maeve dancing and singing as a way to mock her as she is not in her human form," said William.

"Can she not turn herself into a human?" asked Eileen.

"No, she has to summon a spirit that will allow her to, and that is back in the forest in Cirencester," responded William.

"But you still haven't mentioned how you managed to come here?" asked Jasper.

"Right, well, where to begin? There was one night, back in Cirencester, I left home when all were asleep. I made my way to Stonehenge by myself, for the owls were having a secret meeting. They were conversing about Maeve. When they mentioned her, I was excited. After many times I went looking for her in the forest, I would finally know where to find her. I did my best to hide from their sight, but hiding from an owl can be quite difficult. When Socrates discovered my presence, he asked me what I was doing so far from home all by myself so late at night. I told him the truth. I had heard from other animals that there would be a secret meeting. Socrates told me to go back home, but the other owls wanted me to stay," said William.

"What for?" asked Jasper.

"The Covenant and Socrates finally knew where Alistair and Maeve were. But at the time, Alistair had finally secured all the power amongst the animals in London, as he soared through the skies terrorizing and taking whatever he pleased. Animals started to fear him and work for him.

Everyone was too scared. He finally made the Phoenix his lair for him and his thugs. He started to hoard different riches thinking he was a phoenix. But power, fame, and richness weren't enough. He wanted to prove that his ambition had no limits and that no animal would defy him. It was too dangerous for Socrates to go, so the rest of the Covenant thought I could go as a spy. Socrates was against this proposition, but regardless I accepted.

That night I went back home; Socrates kept telling me not to do what the other owls wanted, but I was stubborn and wanted to leave the village. I thought to myself, I will be gone for a couple of weeks and later return as a hero. I wanted adventure, and I would finally meet a druid that would teach me magic. Alistair is no fool, he was expecting someone to come and rescue Maeve, but he never expected a rabbit to do it. So, I gained Alistair's trust by showing him which animals secretly stole from him," said William.

"How did you get caught?" asked Jasper.

"Remember what I said about Mr. Thorn knowing everything that happens here? Well, he does. When I finally met Maeve, I told her who I was. We had planned our escape the night before leaving. We thought the coast was clear, but we were wrong. Mr. Thorn and his thugs were waiting outside for us the moment we stepped out of the Phoenix. Ever since then, I have been under the special watch of Alistair himself.

"I had no idea the Covenant asked you to come here," said Jasper.

"It's not their fault, Socrates tried to stop me, but I was foolish.

"If we get out of here alive, do you think mum would be happy to see me?" asked William.

"Of course, she will."

Both brothers walked and hugged each other very tightly. The bond of brotherhood was reforged, regardless of how a horrendous place they were in. Jasper continued telling William how much the village has changed, of his adventures with Collin, how their mother knows more magic than expected and all kinds of crazy and fun stories that William was unaware of. Collin was starting to feel and was now able to speak. Eileen and Collin joined the conversation with William. They were talking about how beautiful Cirencester continued to be, but also that things have been a bit chaotic in the last couple of days.

After a long night of conversing on the good old days, the four rabbits would soon go to sleep in their small dirty cell and awaits Alistair's decision and what would be done to all four of them.

20 SEPTEMBER 7ᵀᴴ, 1940

THE NEXT DAY, SEPTEMBER 7ᵀᴴ, a couple of hours after midday, Mr. Thorn, accompanied by a group of mean-looking badgers, came to the cells to let the four rabbits know that Alistair wanted to see them.

"Get up! It seems Alistair has decided what to do with you lot. I hope the brotherly reunion was a joyous one," snickered Mr. Thorn.

"You won't get away with this Thorn!" cried Jasper. William tries to calm Jasper.

Mr. Thorn opens the cell door and extends his arm to show where the rabbits have to go.

"You, country vermin, should know I always get away with everything," replied Mr. Thorn. One by one, they left the cell and started to walk towards Alistair's court. Collin had his chest puffed out and had a firm attitude. If today was his last day, he was proud to be alongside his best mate. Eileen was serious and thinking of the different possible outcomes, but if this was her last day of life, she felt she had to say one thing to Jasper.

William was walking tall and strong. If this were his last day, he would have wished to see his mother for one last time. And, as for Jasper, he had no regrets because he promised himself that today would not be his last day.

The four rabbits, Mr. Thorn, and his badgers entered the circular room to see Alistair looking up into the sky. He could feel something brewing.

"Alistair, I brought the prisoners. What would you like me to do with them"? asked Mr. Thorn.

"Just line them up in front of me," said Alistair.

"I'm scared, Jasper, what is the plan? whispered Eileen to Jasper. But he was silent. He did not answer Eileen's question. For he heard nothing, he stared right into Alistair's eye, and Alistair into his. He made a fist with his paw as if ready to strike.

"Jasper, there is something I need to tell you," said Eileen. But Jasper continued to concentrate all of his focus on the falcon.

"Then, what do you plan to do with us?" asked Jasper.

"Well, that's very simple, young Jasper. I intend to eat the four of you right where you stand, starting with your conniving brother for his thievery and treachery!" said Alistair.

"Do what you want to me! But let my brother and the others go!" implored William.

"You have no power here, you scoundrel of a rabbit! I shall do as I please!" said Alistair with a smile.

"What do you plan to do with Maeve?" asked William.

"I suppose I can tell you; consider it as a last request. Mr. Thorn! Bring in the ginger squirrel. I would like her to see what happens to those who try to take her away from the Phoenix," said Alistair.

"Right away, Alistair," responded Mr. Thorn. Mr. Thorn walks back through the long hall in search of Maeve. Meanwhile, Alistair was sharping his claws as he was preparing to slash the four rabbits. Soon you could hear voices struggling in the hallway.

"Get your dirty paws off me! Get away! You hedgehog! Don't touch me!" In comes Mr. Thorn, dragging in Maeve as she tries to push him away.

"That's alright, Mr. Thorn, thank you. It would appear our beloved ginger squirrel is upset. What seems to be the problem? Have we not treated you well?" asked Alistair.

"First of all, do not call me Ginger! That is not my name! And you have me imprisoned here, how do you expect me to react?!"

"That's not the tone of a lady, is it now? Look who we have before us. William the rabbit, the one that tried to take you away from us and the Phoenix, the one who took a hypocritical oath to me and who I mistook for a friend and turned out to be a liar and a thief!" Maeve is looking directly at William. "And his sibling and friends. Do you know what I will do with them?" asked Alistair.

Maeve looked at the rabbits and looked at Alistair. She did not want to answer his question.

"No answer? That's all right. You must be a little shy. I am going to eat them in front of you! So next time you try to escape, you know what happens to those who conspire against me!" said Alistair.

"Why must you be so cruel to animals? What made you like this? Let them go, Alistair, do not do this! I convey you, by the power of Merlin, to let them go, Alistair!" Maeve's voice starts to break, and she feels scared and helpless.

"Merlin?" Laughed Alistair. "Spare me your useless words, for I will send the four of you to oblivion."

As Alistair spreads his wings out, flies towards the rabbits, he lands with both claws on Jasper, Eileen, Collin, and William. Right in that moment of complete helplessness of the rabbits, a very loud sound of a siren roars through the air, and beams of light are directed towards the pitch-dark sky.

"Alistair! I think we need to get out of here. I think the humans are up to something!" said Mr. Thorn.

"Not until I am done with these four parasitic leaches! Mr. Thorn! Don't you dare think of leaving!" replied Alistair in a manic manner. He glides towards the four rabbits and manages to get all four under his claws.

"For the blood of my sacrifice for which you will choke on, you will not get away with this!" said William.

They could feel the weight of the large falcon slowly crushing their bodies. William and Collin fidgeted ferociously under Alistair's feet. Collin even tried biting them, but nothing was working. In a very slow process, the air was diminishing from their lungs. They could not scream from the pain and fear they were living in. Mr. Thorn and his badgers were on the other side of the room, watching impatiently as they wanted to leave.

Even though Jasper had come all this way from his home, he was happy to be with his brother. He was happy he finally found him. He was holding his brother's paw tight as he was being crushed.

He could only hear a faint echo of Mr. Thorn yelling at Alistair that they needed to leave immediately. Jasper's eyesight was now starting to fade. He looked right above him, and he could see Alistair's beak getting closer and closer to William. Jasper heard Alistair say to William, "You have fulfilled your purpose." On the far end of the room, he could see the badgers starting to run away and Mr. Thorn waiving to Alistair. In his mind, he was starting to see his mother, thinking if she would be ok by herself, if she would be proud of him for making this far, and his final thought was if Eileen and Collin would ever forgive him for bringing them to their end. But soon, none of that would matter.

Along with the noise of the sirens coming from London's streets, Jasper could see a large fleet of black planes flying over the city through the hole in the roof. They were dozens, if not hundreds. Close to the planes, small black clouds were exploding around them. What is happening, he thought? He could feel the ground shake and tremble everywhere. The sounds of the ground exploding were constant. Some of the noise was further than others. Regardless, it was nonstop. An orchestra of explosive unholy noise rambled throughout the city.

At that very moment, the most unexpected thing happened. An Austin London Taxicab bursts into the court, breaking down the wall right where Mr. Thorn was standing. Some debris hits Alistair, throwing him to the other side of the room. The whole room is covered in dust, and the four rabbits and Maeve were coughing and trying to figure out what had just happened. Jasper is still very dizzy and tries to stand up, but the headlights from the vehicle are on, and he cannot see who is commandeering the taxi.

"Jasper, what just happened?" asked Collin as he tried to stop coughing.

"I think we are about to find out," said Jasper.

Jasper and Collin start to help the others get up while keeping an eye on the vehicle. William starts to ask Maeve if she is alright. Meanwhile, Eileen, Jasper, and Collin can see the taxi slightly move side to side. The motor is still running, and they are waiting for something to happen. They hear more than one voice from inside the cab as if there was a type of argument. A door opens, the four rabbits and Maeve group together, but instead of witnessing a human coming out of the taxi, it is Jack. Jack and his Pack were the ones driving the car.

21 THE ESCAPE

EILEEN COULDN'T BELIEVE her own eyes. She and the rest did not expect a taxicab to be their salvation.

Jack, Reggie, and Billy walked out of the car. Reggie and Billy were a little rattled up by the impact, but Jack was steady as ever. And of course, Kevin came out of the car very jumpy and happily pouncing on about being in a motor car.

"I'll deal with you in a moment," said Jack to the rabbits. He walks over to where Alistair is lying. He stands right over the falcon's body and looks right at him. Alistair is not moving. The sounds of the blasts and incendiary bombs from outside does bother Jack. "It seems you're struck of luck is over, you oversize hen; and good riddance to you."

Jack turns around, walks away from Alistair, and regroups with his pack waiting beside the car. Jasper can see the four of them talking amongst themselves, but he is unaware of what they are discussing. Jack and his group walk towards the rabbits and Maeve.

"I am overwhelmed stunned to see you, Jack, though I'm not sure if I should be grateful or fearful," said Jasper.

"Calm yourself, rabbit. After what happened in Kemble, you mustn't worry about our presence," replied Jack.

"Oh! How wonderful is it to see you again, my rabbits! How has been your time in London?" asked Kevin in a very cheerful manner.

"Well, otherwise moments from being a falcon's dinner, I'd say quite well. However, we have found whom we came for, and I believe it is time we went back home and quickly," replied Collin.

"How exciting! I thought of all of you and brought some jam roly-poly, knickerbocker glories, bread and butter pudding, and treacle tart. It's all in the motor vehicle!" said Kevin happily.

But their conversation was cut short because incendiary bombs were falling into the Phoenix and had started to flare.

"Ok, you lot, listen here! I will explain everything later! But we must get going before we are cooked in here," said Jack. The four foxes quickly jump into the car and were waiting for the rabbits to come as well.

"What do we do? Do we trust Jack?" asked Eileen.

"I'm not sure; what do you think, Collin?" asked Jasper.

"Oh, let's just get going. It's better than staying in this horrid place," said Collin.

"Wait! What do we do about Alistair?" asked Jasper.

"Leave him, rabbit; he is far gone from this world," said Jack.

"Brother, are you ready to leave?" asked Jasper.

"More than ever! Maeve, let's get going!" said William with much enthusiasm.

"This is it! I'm going back home!" said Maeve. The four rabbits and Maeve quickly jumped into the car with the foxes. Billy and Reggie were on the bottom working on the gas and brake pedal, Kevin was steering, and Jack was indicating where to go. Jasper, William, Eileen, and Maeve went to the back seat and grabbed on whatever they could.

"Kevin, allow me to help you steer! I'm curious to see how this works," said Collin.

"Gladly!"

"Less chatter, you two! We need to leave now!" interrupted Jack.

Collin stands next to Kevin to help with the steering. Jack orders to leave, and Reginald and Billie start to play with the pedals. The car comes out from the building in reverse, and the impact damages the front part of the vehicle. The whistling of bombs falling from the air is eternal, and the car starts to move forward at top speed.

"Do you know where you're going, Jack?!" asked Jasper.

"We are heading west of the city! Heading back to the Cotswold!" Kevin and Collin did an excellent job evading all the holes in the street and the debris exploding from all sides of the road. They could see the buildings around them were starting to catch rapidly on fire. They saw a different version of the humans that were on the street. They were working bravely together, putting themselves in harm's way to put out the fires. They were escorting the elderly and the younger ones to safer zones. Never had the animals seen the humans working together in such a way. However, despite all the heroic efforts, the flames were spreading too fast for them to put out.

The city that William felt was a concrete forest of life and joy was now turning into an inferno. Other humans were too busy trying to reach their bomb shelters that they paid no attention to the taxicab. They were all frightened of the bombs falling. As the bombs came down whistling, the rabbits never knew where they were going to hit.

Jasper and William looked behind from the back window, and they saw a series of bombs falling very near the Phoenix, turning it into rubble. Several large explosive blasts of rock and fire came out, bursting from the ground as the bombs impacted. They could see parts of the Phoenix being engulfed in flames. The ceiling was starting to collapse. The walls were caving in, and the fire started to break the windows from the inside.

Maeve placed her paw on William's shoulder and thanked him for getting her out of the Phoenix.

"We just have to get out of London, and all will be fine," said William.

Jasper observed how his reality was so terribly shocking, and his dream made sense. But before the Phoenix would be destroyed, he saw Alistair rising from the ashes and rubble. With some of his feathers on fire and wearing gold, he almost looked like an actual phoenix. He flew out the hole he had in his court and shrieked so loud that everyone in the vehicle could hear it.

"Blast it! Does he ever stay down?" yelled Jack. With the increasing flames and smoke, and driving through several roads of military checkpoints, making strong turns, they hoped that it would suffice to cover themselves from Alistair's sight. Every building that they drove by was either crumbling or on fire. They all looked towards the sky, and all they could see were the glare of the flames in the night sky.

Alistair has never been more furious in his life. He soared the sky ferociously, trying to locate the vehicle. He would not show mercy. He was out for the hunt. He was out to seek revenge, never has there been an animal as cruel and bloodthirsty as Alistair.

Amid the ravaging chaos London was facing, Alistair was successfully able to locate the vehicle Maeve was in. At this point, they were reaching Trafalgar Square. When the rabbits and Maeve found out he was onto them again, they told Kevin they needed to go faster. Kevin tells his Pack that now they are in for the real deal! The taxicab accelerates, and they see Alistair closing in from the rear-view mirror.

Everyone in the car is yelling that they should be going faster. But then there is an odd noise coming from the engine. Cricking and clanking noises were coming from the engine, making the vehicle go slower. Soon a gush of steam would be coming out of the bonnet. Both Reggie and Billy were playing with the pedals and Jack with the gears to see if anything is happening. As the car starts to slow down, Jack tells everyone to jump ship and run as fast as possible! The car finally stops near the Equestrian Statue of Charles I.

"Everyone out!" cried Jack. Jack and his Pack, the rabbits, and Maeve make their way down through Whitehall Street. Along the street, they make their way into an alleyway that leads to the river Thames with the hope of hiding from Alistair's view. As they walked through the compact street, the sound of the bombing and explosions were not as thundering as it was moments ago. The fire wasn't causing as much damage to the buildings as near Saint Paul's Cathedral. They all walked close to each other, looking in all directions. They can feel, hear and smell burning houses collapsing around them. Buildings made of stone that were erected centuries ago started crumbling down. The sky is filled with black smoke, ash, and red glare. They could hear the sound of planes but not see them.

"We're almost there," said Jasper. As they were starting to walk out the alley, Collin noticed a figure soaring through the smoke.

"I saw that too. We have to keep close," said Eileen. The nine of them are back-to-back, trying to catch with their eye what is flying around them at such a fast speed. The unidentifiable object starts to pick up speed, but no one can see what it is or who it is.

"It's him!" cried Maeve. Jasper looks up and sees that a fire whirl is starting to form right above them. The flying shadow continues to make rapid circles in the sky, and Jasper stares for a while, squinting his eyes until they lock on with Alistair's only eye.

"Run!" cried Jasper. Before anyone could scatter, Alistair swoops down from the sky, striking the foxes with his wings and pecking them with his beak. He grabs Collin and Eileen with his claws and flings them against a burning brick wall. Jasper and William courageously dash towards Alistair. But before they know it, they are again under his pressuring claws where he would, for a second time, try to slowly squeeze every single last breath.

"Now, where were we, boys?" asked Alistair, snickering. And out of the blue, a small stone is flung with much strength into the air and directly hits Alistar's eye. He lets out a horrid shriek of pain that pierced your ears. He lets go of Jasper and William and takes a couple of steps back. Blood has started to drizzle down his eye, and he tries to rub it off with his wing. He could still see, but his vision was impaired. He could see that Maeve was at the very end of the alleyway holding a very sharp piece of fallen glass pointed towards him.

"It is me you want, Alistair! What's the matter?! Are you exhausted? From what? Flying around? You are already burnt and barely have any feathers! You're no phoenix; you're a fool! In the name of Merlin, your tyranny ends here. Come and get me," said Maeve.

If there was any time Jasper thought the world went much slower than usual, it was in that very moment. Jasper saw Alistair's eye, damaged as it was; his eye was filled with hate and anger. He screeched towards Maeve, louder than the one before. He spread out his damaged wings and slowly started to take off from the ground. Jasper looked around him as he was having trouble getting up. To his left, he saw Jack, Billy, and Reggie trying to wake Kevin up, but he was not responding. Jack's tears started to fall on his brother's face. Jack had never felt so helpless ever in his life. No way of helping his brother.

In front of Jasper, Eileen dragged Collin by his collar as the brick wall on fire had started to crumble down.

He also saw his brother alive, but he seemed to be slowly dying from the inside. William had endured far too much in London, he wanted to quit right there at that moment, but he knew Jasper wouldn't let him.

Buildings that were popping, crackling, blowing up, and burning made no difference for Alistair. He, too, was tired from all the chasing and trouble and almost being burnt alive. He just wanted to end things as well. He wasn't planning on taking Maeve back to the Phoenix, for there was no more Phoenix Club, just rubble, dust, and dead memories. No, this would be the end of Maeve, and she knew it. From where Maeve was, she looked at William and Jasper. Not only did she look directly into their eyes but into their souls. And just by mouthing the words, she said, 'thank you, now run.' Jasper and William were getting up. But before he could sprint towards Maeve, Alistair was already flying beak forward with his claws, not to grab her, but to slash her. And Maeve closed her eyes.

Jasper looked up into the sky and saw one of those bombs falling over a building between the distance of Alistair and Maeve.

"Maeve! Maeve! Look out!" cried Jasper. Maeve slightly opens her eyes and sees that Jasper is running behind Alistair and is pointing above the house. She also sees the bomb falling and knows that it will explode. But Alistair does not see it falling. His anger and hatred blind him. She now knows what to do. In a matter of seconds, moments before the bomb impacts the house, everything in Jasper's mind goes silent.

The windows and the walls of the house violently explode everywhere. Rock and rubble are scattered, piercing through the air. The house is engulfed in flames, and the foundation starts to collapse. Alistair is shaken by the explosion and starts to lose control of his flying. His sight is averted from Maeve and directed towards the burning home. He skids on the floor and tries to regain control. He leaps from the floor and lunges towards Maeve, but little did he know, he was unable to push forward. There he stood, flapping his wings, trying to push forward, but he wasn't advancing. He looked down where his chest was, and in his chest was the shard of glass Maeve had in her hand. She had stabbed Alistair.

"Is this how our journey ends, Maeve?" asked Alistair as he looked into her eyes.

"No, this is how yours ends. Mine is just about to start," replied Maeve as she pulls out the glass from his chest.

Jasper and William run towards Maeve. As they approach, they see Alistair lowering his wings. He no longer puts up a fight. He looks towards William.

"It seems the tables have turned. I am powerless now. You and your friends have stripped me from my throne. I wonder what you will do now? Will you walk away and go back to your village? Or will you take my place?" asks Alistair as he bleeds out.

"We should get going, William, come," said Jasper. But William did not budge.

"I know you envied me. Perhaps there's more of me in you than what you think. I could have taught you magic. You could have been my disciple," said Alistair.

William leans into Alistair's face. "There is not enough power and gold in this world for me to want to become similar to you," said William. Alistair smiles and tilts his head, and his whole body lies on the floor.

At that moment, Jack approaches with tears in his eyes and his teeth out. "Where is he? Step aside!" said Jack in an aggressive tone.

"He's gone Jack, it's all over," said Maeve. William and Maeve were holding Jack as he tried to rush over Alistair's body.

"Let me slash his throat! I will chew his beak off!" said Jack.

"Calm yourself, Jack!" said William.

"It's Kevin … he's not getting up. I can't make him get up. He's not moving. I don't know what to do," said Jack.

"Take me to him. There is nothing else to do here. Alistair can no longer hurt us," said Maeve.

The three of them go running to where Billy and Reggie are standing. Eileen and Collin were standing next to them as well.

"Is everyone alright?" asked Maeve.

"I have a broken arm, but I've been through worse. But Kevin he … " Collin could not finish his sentence.

"We will get that fixed, fret not," said Maeve as she made her way to Kevin. There he was, lying on the floor. She examined his body and saw he was severely wounded above his belly. Parts of his white fur were smeared with blood. She also noticed scratch marks around his snout and damaged paws. She gently placed her paws on his head and closed her eyes.

"We believe in you, Maeve, try to summon your healing abilities to save him," said Jasper.

"He is fighting inside to stay alive, but only I can save him. This will require a massive amount of energy on my part," said Maeve. "I will try to harness all that I can."

She sat on both of her knees. She placed her hands palms up and started to rub them against each other, and carefully placed them where Kevin was hurting.

"In the divine name of the goddess who breathes life into us, I consecrate and charge my energy as a magical tool for healing," whispered Maeve.

She would breathe into her palms, rub them together and repeat the same words several times. Over and over, she cast the spell. Everyone was watching her closely, working her magic, expecting a miracle. Jack was very shaky and anxious. Maeve's paws were starting to glow green, something that had never happened since she was turned into a forest animal. As she continued with her spell, Jasper pointed out that some of Kevin's wounds were starting to close. Maeve looked upwards towards the sky and was now gasping for air; she was having trouble breathing. She continued to say the words, but it sounded like she was being choked.

Eileen was going to bring Maeve back from her trance.

"We should stop her! Help her ..." said Eileen in a low voice so Jack could not hear her.

"Let Maeve do her magic. She knows what she's doing," said Jasper.

As more of Kevin's wounds were being healed, he started to have some movement, starting with his legs. Maeve looked as if she was on her last breath, so she inhaled as much air as she could and firmly pressed her paws onto his heart, letting out all of her breath. This caused a reaction to Kevin, for he awoke coughing and gasping for air. Maeve fell onto her back.

"He's back! You bloody did it, you witch of a ginger squirrel!" said Jack as he was overwhelmed with joy! William went over to Maeve to see if she was ok.

"I'll be fine. I just need a moment of rest," said Maeve.

"Where was I, big brother?" asked Kevin as he tried to get up.

"Almost had you as a goner, brother of mine," said Jack.

"Wait? Does that mean you were worried about me? That you missed me? Brother!" said Kevin with much enthusiasm.

"Calm yourself, boy, let's not get carried away here," replied Jack as he tried to maintain an emotionless composure, but deep down inside, he was happy.

"As I hate to interrupt this glorious moment, lads, we must press on before we are all consumed by this surrounding inferno," said Collin to the foxes.

"Right, how is the squirrel doing?" asked Jack.

"She's alright, but we must leave now before anything else happens. I'll help her walk," said William.

Everyone is ready to go. As soon as they all turn to walk towards the bank of the river, they all stop.

"Where is he?" Wasn't he there lying dead?" asked Eileen.

"I saw it with my own eyes. Maeve pierced him right in the chest," said Jasper.

"Who are we talking about?" asked Kevin with a smile.

"Alistair is still around ... isn't he Maeve?" asked Jasper.

"I could feel his heartbeat fade away. I don't know how he's not where I left him," replied Maeve.

"What do we do?" asked Collin.

"We leave London, or we won't get another chance," said Maeve. "I don't have enough magic in me to defend us if he shows up."

22 FROM DESPAIR TO HOPE

EVERYONE HURRIED TO THE BANK of the river as fast as they could. None of them wanted to figure out if Alistair was still there or not. Finally, at the bank of the Thames, William pointed out there was a wooden boat on the shore where they could go in and, with it, row back home.

"I wish we could go back in one of those 'automobiles', quite extraordinary invention, but I suppose a wooden boat shall do," said Collin.

"It's not the time to be posh, quickly everyone in," said Jasper.

William was the first one in and helped the ladies climb in and Collin.

"Jasper, you're next. I can't wait to see mum again," said William.

"Coming, I'm just waiting for the foxes," said Jasper. The four foxes calmy sat afar from the rabbits as they saw them getting in the wooden rowboat.

"We're not coming along, Jasper," said Jack.

Jasper and everyone on the boat are shocked to hear this. "You are choosing to stay? For what? Look at the city. It is up in flames. There is nothing else to stay for," said Jasper.

"Though the city is on fire, this is London. And this is our city. And it will strive on," said Jack.

"But what about Alistair? Maybe he is still out there."

"Perhaps, but he no longer has the Phoenix, nor the animals that followed him, and neither Mr. Thorn. He is all by himself. The Pack and I decided that we need to be sure that he is gone for good."

"Please do take care of yourselves."

"Don't worry about us, be sure to know that if you ever come back to London, you have friends here. Now float along back home. It better if you were on your way, Jasper," said Jack.

Jasper hopped into the boat with the rest. The foxes walked towards the side of the boat and, with their heads, they pushed it into the water.

"Goodbye, Collin! Bon voyage! Safe travels! I do hope to see you again soon!" yelled Kevin.

"I hope our paths can meet in the near future! Take care!" replied Collin as he waved towards the foxes.

There they sat, in silence, exhausted and overwhelmed, knowing that it was over. As the boat continued on the river, Jasper and the rest could see Jack, Kevin, Billy and Reggie walk back into the alley from where they came from until they were no longer visible.

From a distance, they could still hear and see the explosions in central London. The city glowed from the very fire that was consuming it. They worried about the humans that were suffering from the bombing. They realized that humans and animals could work together and thrive in times of despair and crises to overcome any obstacle that may appear. The sheer courage and commitment that was shown to put out the fires, fight off the enemy and protect their loved ones all at the same time showed valour in the humans. As the boat continued its course, everyone was grateful to have escaped the furnace they were in.

"What now?" asked Eileen.

"Now, dear Eileen, sit down and relax and think of the west country's beautiful green hills and its fair weather.

The first thing I want to do arriving home is savouring a pint of cider and feel the love and warmth of my mother's embrace," said William.

"I believe I can speak for everyone here, but I think that is all we want," said Eileen.

"I want to go home, smoke my special blend of tobacco, have a glass of wine. ¡No! Two bottles of wine, that is, and sleep in for three days," said Collin as he offered some of the pastries that Kevin brought for them.

"I want to go home and just get back to reality. I think we've all had enough of adventure for now," said Jasper.

"I want to go back into my hut in the forest and be amongst nature once more," said Maeve.

"Will you turn back into your druid self?" asked William.

"I think so, but I need Socrates for that," replied Maeve.

"Why Socrates?" asked William.

"Let's talk about this later, lad, I'm a bit tired from all this, yeah?"

"Of course," said William.

Moments later, the sun was rising. They passed Lambeth, and it was safe to relax a bit. The five of them decided that if they needed to nap, now was the time for it. After all, they all deserved it.

23 HOME

WHEN EVERYONE ON BOARD the boat woke up, they realized they were still floating in the outskirts of London. As they basked under the sun and fair weather, they all thought about how long it would take for them to arrive home.

"When do you reckon we'll see Cirencester again?" asked Eileen.

"At this rate, I'm not too sure. We arrived at London by train, so it's hard to tell," replied Jasper.

In the far end of the boat, Maeve was just waking up. She yawned and stretched her arms in a very cheerful manner.

"Good morning, Maeve, you are in a joyful mood," said Jasper.

"Indeed I am; indeed I am, Jasper. And I will tell you why, at last, I am free again. If it wasn't for you, I thought I would have never escaped London."

"Well, I'm happy to have gotten you and my brother out."

"Anyways." Maeve smacked her knees and got up. She walked towards Eileen and Jasper as she continued to stretch. "What is our current situation?"

"We seem to be moving a lot slower than what I expected. We are barely in the outskirts of London, and we can still see the smoke from here," said Jasper.

"Right, well, I have just the thing that can get us home faster." Maeve searched in her satchel for goodies and surprises. Out from it, she took out a small jar that contained a strange white sparkling light. Inside of it, it looked like a willow-o-wisp. "This is our way home," said Maeve.

"What is it?" asked Eileen very curiously,

"This is what we druids call a 'spark in the sky.' I was able to make this when I was imprisoned at the Phoenix. Have you ever seen a firework? Well, essentially, it has the same purpose, only that it is used just for emergencies and I can give it directions. I just have to say an incantation, release the spark, and hopefully, Socrates will know what it is," said Maeve.

"And if doesn't?" asked Jasper.

"Pray that he does, or else we are going to be in this boat for a rather long time," Maeve whispered her incantation to the jar, opened the lid, and the small ball of light went out, shooting straight up towards the sky.

24 THE RESCUE

AFTER THE GREEN and orange explosion in the sky, everyone expected some immediate reaction. But nothing happened. It was a delightful sight, though it lasted shortly.

"What now?" asked Collin.

"Now we wait," said Maeve.

Hours passed by and time felt still sitting in that boat. The weather was fair, but the sense of boredom was stirring up. Collin told some stories of adventures he had shared with Jasper when they were younger to pass the time. As entertaining as they were, there getting repetitive.

"Easy on the stories Collin, I think the rest heard enough of our adventures," said Jasper.

"Indeed, I'm sure I will be hearing much more once I get home," said William.

"If only we had a pint, a lager, an ale, a cider, that is what I miss from home," said Collin.

"Believe it or not, Collin, but it seems that all your wishes are about to come true," said Maeve as she pointed out into the sky.

High above, soaring towards the small wooden boat, was a flock of very distinguished owls.

"Socrates ... " said Jasper.

"It appears so," said Maeve.

Socrates and his companions were closing in on a steady speed. Everyone in the boat was delighted to see friendly faces after their ordeal in London. William started to steer the boat to land gently by the river bank. There is where the owls landed.

"We flew as fast as we could when we saw the explosion in the sky. I knew it could only mean one thing," said Socrates.

"Surely you could have arrived sooner," said Maeve in a sarcastic tone.

"My dear Maeve, it brings joy to my heart to see you again," replied Socrates.

Maeve gets off the boat, walks towards Socrates, and gives him an embracing hug. Socrates covers her with his wings.

"It's all over, Maeve. You are safe now," said Socrates silently.

The rabbits stayed in the boat as they watched Maeve and Socrates exchange words. They couldn't hear what they were saying, but they knew it was good news by looking at their expression.

"Come forward, rabbits, don't think I have forgotten about you," said Socrates.

Jasper, Eileen, Collin, and William get off the boat and walk towards the owls. Socrates takes a good long look at them from head to toe. He finally walks over towards William.

"William, I am sorry for all the pain and suffering you went through. I should not have let you go to London alone. I cannot start to imagine the torment Alistair put you through. I apologize to all of you, and especially to you, Maeve. I—"

"Socrates, please, I am pleased to see you again, but it was my decision to leave the village. I went against your warnings. I wanted an adventure, and I got exactly that, and Alistair is no more," said William.

"I understand, William. Now to have a word with these three mischievous rabbits that left the village placing their very lives in danger and leaving without letting anyone know, and in the middle of a war!" Socrates puffed out his chest and looked downwards towards Jasper, Eileen, and Collin. "Thank you, thank you for rescuing Maeve, and you have shown courage, commitment, and brotherly love. You have shown bravery, Jasper Jones," said Socrates.

"Ahem! What about us?!" asked Collin interruptingly.

"Jasper is very lucky in having two lion-hearted companions. Without you two, who knows what could have happened," said Socrates. Collin was very gratified to know that Socrates recognized him.

"Socrates, sir, what happens now? Will you take us back to Cirencester?" asked Eileen.

Socrates stood silent for a moment and cleared his throat. "Cirencester and the surrounding areas have been bombed, and much has changed.

"And the forest?" asked Eileen.

"Parts of the forest have taken severe damage, but it is not safe for humans nor animals to stay in the area," said Socrates.

"But what about the underground tunnels? Surely we can stay there," said Collin.

"The tunnels were safe for a while, but the bombing continued, some of the tunnels collapsed, there was not enough space for everyone," said Socrates.

"Then, where is everyone else? Where did they go to?" asked Jasper.

"I commanded the owls and birds to carry the young ones up north to Scotland, far from the cities and the shores of Wales. Where there are no humans, where they can be safe. The rest, we sent them to Oxford," said Socrates.

"Why Oxford?" asked Eileen.

"For some reason, it has not been severely damaged as other villages. Also, there are several places where we can take refuge. There are nearby forests and underground human-made tunnels," said Socrates. "Some of us have stayed in Cirencester in case you were to be able to make a signal of your return, which you have," added Socrates.

"I see … and my mother, is she alive?" asked Jasper.

"She is my boy, and so is yours, Eileen." She gave a sigh of relief when she heard this. "But we must press on. First, we must take Maeve to Cirencester so she can take the form of her natural self, druid."

Socrates and the other owls grabbed Maeve and the rabbits with their claws and started to fly towards Cirencester.

"The forest is not the same as the last time you saw it, Maeve," said Socrates as they were soaring into the air.

"Don't worry, I might have the trick up my sleeve to make it better," replied Maeve.

Jasper, Eileen, William, and Collin have never been picked up by an owl. It was their first time feeling the rush of wind into their faces. The experience was heart-felt and thrilling, but it had to be cut short. As they flew out of a cloud into the open, from high above, everyone could see craters on the ground caused by the bombing. The earth was already torn and scorched by the ungodly acts of war. Never has Jasper seen England's soft and curvy green hills in a state of deformity. He could only think what home could look like. At that moment, he thought of his mother. A sentiment of concern and uneasiness started to build up inside of him. Happy as he was with being alongside his brother, thinking about his mum Catherine weighed heavily on his mind and in his heart.

25 THE RITUAL

THE OWLS WERE APPROACHING the forest of Cirencester. Much of the land was already damaged. The trees and branches have fallen over and scattered. There is still green and vegetation in the area, but it is not the same as before Jasper left for London.

"Who would do such an unholy act onto the forest?" asked Eileen.

"Humans, my dear, humans. They have the power to create marvellous things, to make breaking discoveries, but sadly, some still act like brutes and savages using the part of the mind for destruction," said Maeve as they were landing in the middle of the forest.

"Where exactly are we?" asked Jasper.

"We are where I met your mother many years ago. I look forward to seeing her again," said Maeve.

They landed in an open area of the forest. The sense of life and vitality of the forest was dull. The grass was not very green, and a feeling of sombreness surrounded the environment.

"I never thought I see my home with such sadness," said Maeve. She saw the very same trunk where Catherine and Janice were taking refuge many years ago. Everything around her seemed very nostalgic.

"Jasper, did you know the trees can talk?" said Maeve.

"Talk, how? I've spent all my life in the forest, and never have I heard a word from them," replied Jasper.

"They speak amongst themselves, through the roots that are deep into the ground. Sometimes I can hear what they say. They are old souls. They have lived for many years and seen many things."

"And can you hear what they're saying now?" asked Jasper. Maeve closed her eyes and took a deep breath in.

"I can. They're saying that a tremendous amount of pain has stained this place. The forest has been scarred and wants to be healed again. It is my job to revive this forest. I will not see it be destroyed any longer. Socrates, let's commence the ritual now!" said Maeve.

"What ritual?" asked Jasper.

"Cernunnos. I need all you to stand back," replied Maeve.

Jasper did as he was told and took several steps back. Everyone gave her the space she needed. Maeve, from her pouch, took out a green powder and made a circle on the ground for her to kneel in the centre. She then took out two flint stones and struck them together by the powder so they could catch on fire. Successfully the powder caught flame, and a circle of fire was created.

Jasper asked Socrates what Cernunnos is, and he responded that Cernunnos is the Celtic god of the forest and was the only one that could break her curse. Maeve was now kneeling in the middle of the circle and was motionless. She took several breaths and started with the prayer.

> Ancient God of the forest deeps,
> master of beast and sun,
> here where the world is hushed and sleeps,
> now that the day is done.
> I call you in an ancient way,

here in my circle round,
asking that you will hear me pray
and send your sun force down.

Maeve repeated the prayer out loud several times, each time with more passion, and each time the flame was getting bigger and bigger until it became like a dome, and she was no longer visible.

"We have to get her out of there. She's going to die in the flame!" said William.

"NO! We mustn't interrupt the ritual. She knows what she is doing," said Socrates.

The flame continued to grow and was almost as tall as a house. No one could hear what Maeve was saying. The only thing that could be heard was the flow and flicker of the fire. Right above the flame, a green spirit-like figure appeared. He was a man that shared features that of a fallow deer. He had pointy ears, long brown hair, a short beard, deer horns, and deer eyes. The upper half of his body resembled that of a human. He was partially covered in leaves and vines. His lower half resembled that of a deer. He was holding an arm ring in his left hand and, in his right, a serpent-shaped staff.

"What is happening?" asked Eileen.

"Maeve is asking for permission and help from Cernunnos to return to her human form," said Socrates.

Cernunnos did not say a word. He only looked into the middle of the fire where Maeve sat. As he closed his eyes, the flame exploded into a blinding white light, and everyone had to cover their eyes, and a strong gush of wind followed.

After the explosion, everyone blinked and rubbed their eyes, trying to get their normal sight back. Although their vision was momentarily blurry, Jasper could see that the green powder circle was no longer there in the middle. He saw a human dressed in light brown robes.

"Jasper, can you see anything? Is Maeve alright?" asked Collin.

"My hazy vision is starting to wear off. I think I see someone."

The human that was before them started walking towards the animals. And knelt.

"I'm back."

"Maeve? Is that really you?" asked Jasper. He was amazed to see the most beautiful druid ever. Her long locks of red hair and porcelain skin were back. Her captivating face has never been as divine and enthralling as that day.

"I'm no longer the squirrel you met in London. I've returned to my original form," said Maeve.

At that moment, the animals had fully regained their sight and could look at the prepossessing Maeve. Everyone took a good glance at her. Never have they a seen a human that resembled the heavens so, and her eyes golden were brighter than any star in the sky.

"Maeve, I see the ritual was a success. It is good to have you back to your original self," said Socrates.

"Maeve, how are you feeling?" asked William.

"I feel well, thank you. Thanks to you, I'm back home, and thanks to your brother, we've both made it home."

"Did the spirit say anything to you?" asked Jasper.

"He did," said Maeve. "I was able to turn back into my druid self so I could restore the balance of forest, revive this place to its magical and vibrant green way it once was. It would seem I have a lot of work to do."

"What does this mean? Will we not see you again?" asked Eileen.

"Not at all. The four of you have to go with Socrates until the war ends, you know where to find me, and I will always be here for you. But I need to stay here and heal this forest. This is not farewell, but I can no longer accompany you to where you have to go, for my place is here, in the forest," said Maeve.

"We understand, Maeve, thank you," said William with a breaking voice.

"No, thank you for everything. You were very brave. I'm sure our paths will come across again; for the meantime, I give you all my blessing," replied Maeve. She said a small prayer of prosperity and abundance to the four of them. When she was done, she signalled Socrates and the other owls it was time for her to return deep into the forest.

"Come along, rabbits, we need to take you Oxford. Your families are waiting for you there," said Socrates. When he and the other owls got a hold of the rabbits, they started to take off. As they were getting higher and higher, Jasper and William looked back at the forest and could see Maeve walking into the trees, followed by a strong mist that covered her until she completely disappeared.

26 OXFORD

IN THE OUTSKIRTS OF OXFORD, there was a forest that was big enough for the animals to take refuge until the war passed. When Jasper, William, Eileen, and Collin arrived, they came soaring down, flown by the owls. The animals of the forest had gotten word that the four mischievous rabbits had returned and brought back William.

The moment they touched the ground, all of the animals—of all kinds—came out of their homes to greet them and treat them as heroes. The word got out that Jasper and his friends travelled far to rescue his brother. Everyone was excited to see the four rabbits return home. Many questions were asked about their adventure, what they saw, and if they were hungry.

"I didn't expect to see everyone so happy," said Jasper.

"Last time you saw the village, they were at each other's throats. But in dire times, everyone finds a way to support each other," replied Socrates.

"Where are our families?" asked Eileen.

"Ah, there they are," said Socrates.

Amongst the crowd of animals that were celebrating the return of Jasper, Eileen, Collin, and William, came the families of the rabbits. Sarah was fully recovered, and she ran to her daughter to give her the biggest hug she had ever received in her life. Collin's family had food and beer for their young explorer. He, too, was given a grand hug.

"I'm nervous," said William as he looked at Jasper. "What if our mother doesn't recognize me? Or doesn't want anything to do with me and throws me out."

"Calm yourself, brother. There's no need to be on the defensive. You are back home," replied Jasper.

Catherine finally comes forward, and she is wearing her kitchen clothes. She slowly walks towards her sons and gently places her paw on Jasper's face then on William's. She is speechless, but her heart is racing with joy and content. Before she can say anything, she strongly hugs both of her sons, squeezing the air out of them.

"Welcome home, boys," said Catherine. "The best gift a mother can have is knowing her two boys are safe."

"It's good to be back home," said Jasper.

William is still nervous and doesn't know what to say. As he tries to say something, nothing comes out of his mouth.

"It's alright, dear, you survived, whatever differences we had in the past, stays in the past, and you have made it home thanks to your brother. Come along, let's have something to eat," said Catherine.

William and Catherine were given space to catch up while the three rabbits stood by. They all looked at each other and smiled. They were happy to be back home with their family and friends.

Collin could sense some traction between Eileen and Jasper and knew this was the moment to give them space as well.

"I guess this all this goes into our list of adventures, eh, Jasper. Maybe we will get to hear those songs and stories about us. Well, I don't know about you two, but I'm going to find a pub and get that wine. I will see you all later in the evening," said Collin happily as he left Jasper and Eileen to themselves.

Jasper and Eileen saw Collin walk off.

"You know, back in London, there were times that I felt it was going to be the end, and I'm happy we all made it out alive," said Jasper.

"I'm happy as well, we live to see another day," replied Eileen with a smile.

"Since we left Cirencester, I couldn't stop wondering, was there something you wanted to say to me back in London?" asked Jasper nervously.

Eileen smiles and blushes. She wanted to confess her feelings for Jasper. She stands on her tippy toes and gives a tender kiss to Jasper on the cheek.

Jasper stands there with his eyes wide open, with a sense of euphoria overwhelming him.

"I will tell you later, Jasper. For now, I need to rest," said Eileen happily.

"Of course, I will see you all later," replied Jasper.

Later that evening, after Jasper, William, Eileen, and Collin were telling their adventure in London to everyone and their families, Socrates arrived at Jasper's new house.

They were in an open field having tea, discussing what it's like to be in Oxford, and that they met a family of rats on the train to London and that they live somewhere in town. As they had their tea, they wondered whether they would ever go back to Cirencester.

"So, you brought Maeve back to the forest, how is she?" asked Catherine.

"Indeed, we did, she says she hopes to see you again," replied William

"Well, everything in due time. I'm sure I'll see her again soon too. She's a very powerful druid, you know," said Catherine.

"Now tell me, Jasper, what do you know of Alistair? Did he perish, or is he still around?" asked Socrates.

"I'm not sure. He was struck in the chest with a shard of glass and fell on the floor. He stopped moving. We thought he was gone; we went to help a friend who was hurt. But when we turned our backs, he was no longer there. It's like if he disappeared."

"I see. This is what I feared. You see, Alistair is a vile creature. It is a miracle and a blessing that you all four and Maeve survived," said Socrates.

"If he's still out there, do you think he will return?" asked Jasper.

"There is no way of knowing for sure, as long as Maeve is here and she continues to guard the forest and its creatures, Alistair is no match for her," replied Socrates.

"So, are we safe?" asked Jasper.

"For the time being, yes, we are," replied Socrates.

"Will we ever go back to Cirencester?" asked William.

"I believe so. As destructive as it is, this war of man will not last forever. We will return home one day. Meanwhile, we stay here, where it is safe," said Socrates.

Later that night, Jasper, William, and Catherine all walked towards the hut they were staying in on the outskirts of Oxford. They had a marvellous time outside and looked forward to doing it tomorrow. They never thought they would enjoy the moment of just them three having tea and cake in the beautiful Oxford. Catherine had some alone time with William because they needed to catch up plenty. Jasper watched as his brother and mother conversed joyfully, and was grateful he was back home.

Jasper made his way to his bed, changed into his sleeping clothes, and stretched his arms up high as he was ready to go to sleep. He sat in his bed thinking of everything that had happened. Everything from the summer solstice to this moment.

It was the first time in a while that he was sleeping in the comfort of his new home. He had forgotten the smell and the feel of soft sheets and warm blankets, and it was heavenly. He laid back his head onto the pillows and prayed for a peaceful sleep and peaceful dreams, that his visions this time would be pleasant and relaxing. Jasper slowly closed his eyes, and off he was into dreamland.

27 SURVIVAL

BOMBS CONTINUED TO FALL on London; there was no knowing when the ruination of the city would stop. The sounds of the ferocious blasts and explosions echoed throughout the night. Many humans have sought refuge below the surface, avoiding the city's wrecking. The London Underground became a second home for the humans as they slept on platforms, trains, and stations. The conditions there were far from suitable: it was cold, smelly, overcrowded, and damp. However, they did their best to keep morale high through songs and unity.

Deep in the underground, far away from the humans, Mr. Thorn was dragging the body of Alistair.

"I told you, we should've left when we had the chance," said Mr. Thorn silently.

Mr. Thorn had massive strength for a hedgehog, but dragging Alistair was no easy task. He had found a remote location deep underground where the humans would not disturb them. He had a small kit that contained notes and small jars of ancient herbs and medicines with him. When he opened the kit, he carefully examined his notes one by one.

"If you think you were the only one who knew magic in the Phoenix, let me tell you how wrong you were," said Mr. Thorn.

Alistair mumbled something that could not be understood.

"Save your breath, for what I am about to do will benefit us both, well, mainly me," said Mr. Thorn.

He opened his jars and rubbed the herbs and ointments on his wound. Then he grabbed his notes and recited what was written on them. He repeated a spell to heal Alistair and relieve him from his suffering.

As Mr. Thorn read the words written on his notes, Alistair started to moan and groan louder. Mr. Thorn's spell was bringing back Alistair, but it was also causing him great pain in the process. When the ritual was over, Alistair's eyes went from golden yellow to a dark blue. He flapped his wings and stood on two feet, and released a retched shriek that echoed in the Underground.

Alistair was back.

ABOUT THE AUTHOR

R.J. QUILANTAN was born to Mexican parents in Milan, Italy, in 1990. He was brought up in a diplomatic family where he has had the opportunity to live and travel to different countries and learn about different cultures around the world.

From Milan to San Antonio, Texas to Hong Kong, and from consulates to state universities to non–profits he has worked in both the private and public sectors.

He showed interest in expressing his creativity by making illustrations and music at a young age. He would later be involved in working in several short films and writing scripts as a hobby where he would discover the art of storytelling. Cinema being one of his many passions, he visualises his writing as if it was a film.

His stories are influenced by real-life experiences, world travels, movies, other literary works, and his imagination. R.J. wants to convey to his readers the emotions he has felt, the wonders he has seen, and the adventures he has been on.

The influence of this novel comes from his experiences in the United Kingdom, specifically in southern England. R.J. Quilantan currently lives in Vancouver, Canada, where he continues to be influenced by life.

Made in the USA
Monee, IL
10 June 2022

fd72499a-3d60-472b-b710-a724a9a82546R01